Righteous Defender

(A Michael Ayers Legal Thriller)

By: O. R. Johnson

Righteous Defender. Copyright © 2017 by O. R. Johnson.

Published by B.O.Y. Publications, Inc.
P.O. Box 1012
Lowell, NC 28098

This book is an original publication of the author who wrote the story herein contained.

Printed in the United States of America

ISBN: 978-0-692-85993-3

Dedication

To my daughters...if you never remember anything else
I teach you, please remember your life is yours alone.
Live and experience everything God has for you while
on this earth. Time here is short...don't waste it! I love
you deeply!

Acknowledgements

For me, writing acknowledgements is one of the hardest parts of writing a book. So many people have encouraged me since I became a writer, and I hate the idea of name dropping and leaving someone out. My remedy for this is the following disclaimer: I am grateful for every word of encouragement, and every reader that has purchased my work and helped to spread the word about my stories. I'm grateful beyond words for the support of my family, friends, classmates, and internet friends that I have connected with via social media. You all make every release a highly-anticipated event and push me to make sure I am releasing my best work. I sincerely love you guys and I wouldn't be able to live my dream without you.

A special thanks goes to three of my dear friends that hold me accountable, challenge me to grow, support my every move, push me to reach my dreams, inspire me to become a better woman, and love me unconditionally; Charita, Ingrid, and Chandrika. You ladies each show me a different piece of myself while sharing your lives with me and inspiring me to continue on this journey. I truly love and respect each of you. Thanks for accepting my silly, my aggressive, my fatigue, my passion, my honor, my worth, and my flawed character. Most of all, thanks for allowing me to be me and not expecting anything of me except what you give me...real sisterhood.

To my children, I've lived my life trying to make sure you lived a childhood you wouldn't need to recover from. I pray you look back with fond memories and hold the life lessons we've poured into you close to your hearts. Omari, Abriah, Adonis, and Elijah...thank you for making my job as your mother relatively easy. You four grew within me, yet your lives nurtured the best parts of me. The world expected one thing, but together we proved that anything is possible when priorities are in the right place. I love you with a love that can't be explained. I don't deserve you, but I'm grateful God gave me the opportunity to grow up right along with you. Ijanee, Eric, and Janae, each of you allowed me into your hearts when I met and married your fathers. You didn't have to accept me. You didn't have to allow me to love you, but you did and I am forever grateful for your presence in my life. I admire each of you. My heart swells with love and pride at the sight of you. You are beautifully gifted souls and I can't wait to see your final product. You've added a richness to my life that has forever changed me. Thank you.

To my parents, brothers, grandparents, aunts, and uncles; thank you for loving a little girl with a big imagination and even bigger mouth (lol). Thank you for your life lessons, your encouragement, your support, your love, your care, your sacrifices, and your prayers. I am who I am because I am little pieces of greatness from each of you.

To my favorite miracle, my lover, my best friend, my biggest encourager, my backbone, my partner in inspiration and in life; Lyndell Johnson you are my absolute. You center me in a way I never thought possible. I cry tears of joy when I think back over my life before and after you. The difference is like night and day. You love me so deeply, that it became contagious and I began to love myself the same way. I would not be who I am without you. I will never be able to repay you for what your love has given me, but I'll spend the rest of my life trying.

Righteous Defender

(A Michael Ayers Legal Thriller)

Prologue

"Evan! Evan wake up," I hear my wife yell as she shakes me. I hear her but everything is still so foggy. And my head is pounding. The aspirin I took before laying down is doing nothing to stop the searing migraine.

"Come on Evan. I'm going to be late for work. I need you to finish feeding the baby. She's in her high chair."

I hear my wife speaking to me, but she sounds so far away. I pry my tired eyes open but the morning light causes jolts of pain to shoot through my skull. I raise my hand to shield my eyes from the light.

"Don't tell me you're hungover again Evan. You promised you'd stop drinking so much."

I want to tell my wife I haven't had anything to drink all week but my mouth doesn't work. I focus on forming the words, but my lips feel like they're sealed shut. I shake my head slowly trying to remove the cobwebs but they don't budge.

"Evan, are you awake? Do you hear your daughter screaming?"

Lisa's words feel like knives stabbing my brain. I nod my head gently just to get her to stop talking. I slide the covers off of me and stand so that she can see I'm awake. The room spins but I manage to remain upright.

"Are you sure you're okay? I really have to get out of here. I can't be late today."

"I'm okay," I manage to force out as my wife turns to rush out of the room. I'm not even sure if she heard me.

I focus on putting one foot in front of the other as I make my way from our bedroom to the kitchen where I hear my daughter whimpering. She's gnawing mercilessly on her fingers as I pull out a chair and sit directly in front of her. I pick up the bowl of baby cereal and concentrate on getting the food out of the bowl and into my daughter. I work slowly but steadily, successfully getting about half of the contents of the bowl into her mouth. My head is still pounding. I close my eyes for a second to try to get a little relief. When I re-open them, I notice my peripheral vision is fading. I can see my daughter clearly but everything around me seems to be going dim. Something is wrong and I need to get my daughter back to her crib while I still can.

I stand very slowly, silently praying I won't fall out while I'm walking. Once upright I pick my daughter up out of her seat and hug her close to my chest. I pick up the bowl and place it in the sink. Out of habit, I turn the water on allowing the bowl to fill with water. I walk my daughter to her crib and lay her down. I feel relief wash over me as I put her pacifier in her mouth. Regardless of what happens to me from here on out, I'm happy knowing my daughter is safe. I walk into my bedroom in search of the phone so I can call 911. I make it to the bedside table before the pain shoots through me again and everything goes dark.

Chapter 1
Ryan

I am jolted out of my sleep by the weight of my two year old as she jumps on my chest and yells, "Daddy, it's wake up time." I want to be sullen but it's difficult to sulk when one is given the opportunity to be awakened by the object of his affection. I have never been much of a morning person. During the first three years of our marriage my wife Janice tried various tactics including sex to lure me out of my cocoon, but nothing ever worked until the birth of our daughter Kaitlin. Kaitlin was just six months old when Janice realized our daughter had the power to wake me with the slightest taps of her chubby little fingers. I wanted to be mad at my wife for manipulating me with our daughter, but the fact was I loved seeing our daughter's face first thing in the morning. She was a lovely reminder of what true love could create. Janice and Kaitlin are the best parts of me and the reason I get up every morning and go to a job I loathe. Although I am still not a morning person, Kaitlin makes getting up much easier. I grab my daughter and pull her close to me. She squeals the high pitched squeal that always puts a smile on my face. If I wasn't completely awake before, I definitely am now.

"Up Daddy! Mommy made pannycakes."

I smile again at my daughter's attempt at saying pancakes. It happens to be one of my favorite mispronunciations which is a difficult title to achieve as Kaitlin has so many. "Tell Mommy Daddy is going back to sleep. No pannycakes for me," I say as I attempt to pull the covers back over my head. Kaitlin is known amongst our family members for her stubborn streak, so I know she will not go away easily. She reaches out and grabs the covers attempting to keep my face exposed.

"No Daddy, Kaitlin is hungry. Come eat with Kaitlin."

Another smile tugs at the corners of my mouth. Yet another thing I find absolutely fascinating about my daughter. She refers to herself in third person. Janice always corrects her. I enjoy it because it reminds me that my baby girl is still a baby girl. I am not anxious to see her grow up. Kaitlin leans over and kisses my cheek. Sometimes I think my wife gives her lessons on how to wake me because she seems to know exactly what to do each morning. Her kiss does the trick.

"Daddy is awake now Sweetie. Go wait for me in the kitchen. I will be down to have breakfast with you in a few minutes."

"Otay." Feeling good about accomplishing her mission Kaitlin turns and climbs down off of the king sized bed. I am amazed at how good she is at climbing on and off of things. It seems like only yesterday I was bringing her home from the hospital and struggling to hold her the proper way. She is growing before my eyes, a thought that makes me call out to her.

"Kaitlin," I yell before she exits the room. Kaitlin turns around to look at me.

"Yesh?"

"Who's Daddy's favorite?"

"Meeee," she squeals before running back in my direction. I hop out of bed and grab her as soon as she is within arm's reach. I scoop my precious girl into my arms and hug her close.

"Wub you Daddy," Kaitlin says before she begins to wiggle her way out of my arms. That's always my cue to release her. Kaitlin loves affection, but only on her terms. I silently pray for her future husband because whoever he is, he better be ready to give my little princess whatever she wants. The more I learn about her personality the more I see she will be a force to be reckoned with one day.

"I love you too sweetie," I say to an empty room as Kaitlin has already started running toward the kitchen to deliver her report to her mother. "I swear those two are in cahoots against me," I whisper to myself as I drag my tired bones towards the shower. My wife knows me well, so I know I have about 15 minutes to shave, shower, throw something on, and head down for breakfast. I look into the mirror and notice the faintest appearance of stubble. I decide I will skip the shave today. I have no court appearances and none of my clients will care if I am not perfectly clean shaven. There was a time when I took pride in my appearance because of my profession. Now the job is simply a means to gain experience and provide for my family.

I am a defense attorney. More accurately, I am a lowly attorney employed by the public defender's office. The pay is terrible and I often defend people that are not too fond of the legal system. I have defended a few innocent people that were arrested and charged by an overzealous police force and politically motivated prosecutor, but those cases are few and far between. Those are the cases that made me want to become a defense attorney. The cases that involved innocent people that deserved a fair trial, fueled by the facts of the case rather than personal vendettas or biases, are the ones that get my blood pumping. Somehow I'm seeing less and less of those coming across my desk and more and more that involve petty repeat criminals being charged with the same insignificant crimes. I fight for them to the best of my ability, only for them to serve a year or less then return to working for the real criminals that should have been arrested in the first place. I shake my head in disgust. My morning pep talk was going to need some work if I was going to survive the next year in my current position. Janice and I have a plan. We have almost saved enough to execute the idea that will transform our lives. "Just twelve more months," I tell myself before slipping into the shower.

The water is cool but not cold. I've never been a fan of piping hot showers, especially during the summer. I like to have the water just cool enough to shock my senses into full alert. I've never been a fan of long laborious showers. To me, a shower is a menial task to complete before donning clothes. To Janice the shower is a luxurious oasis. Since we never leave the bed at the same time, we never have to argue when getting ready in the morning. If for some reason we did need to get ready around the same time, I am always in and out before she ever needs to complain. Today is no different. After a quick wash, rinse, and repeat I step out of the shower, dry off, and go back into the bedroom to put on whatever clothes Janice left out for me. Yes, my wife picks out my clothing. It's not because I am some barely competent man that can't do anything for himself, it's because my wife is a lover of all things fashionable. All things would definitely include me. Janice works as an event planner and plans our lives very similarly to the way she plans events for her high paying clients. She often says she enjoys planning because it helps her keep chaos under control. I secretly believe she just likes dressing me up as though I'm an over grown Ken doll, but I always receive compliments on the ensembles she puts together and seeing me in certain styles sends her hormones into overdrive. The way I see it, I come out on top in every way.

Today's choice of clothing includes a chocolate brown suit paired with a light blue shirt and a chocolate tie with thin light blue stripes. The suit looks vintage, almost like something gangsters wear in the movies. It definitely does not scream lawyer, but neither does anything else my wife picks out. Janice has an eye for style that would be better suited for celebrities than me, but again it makes her happy and gets her libido going so I don't complain.

I quickly dress and make my way downstairs to the kitchen just as Janice is pulling the sausage out of the oven. I catch a glimpse of her ass and wish inwardly that Kaitlin was still asleep. I remember the early years of our marriage when I would practically assault Janice on the kitchen counter before we both headed out to work. My appetite for my wife is insatiable. Janice turns and catches me admiring her. She gives me a naughty smile as she approaches me and throws her arms around my neck.

"Good morning my handsome lover," she purrs as she presses herself into me and kisses me with her full lips.

I enjoy the feel of her against me as my member begins to come awake in anticipation of what's to come. When she releases my lips my eye lids feel weighted. I know I have to regain control, not only for the sake of our wide awake daughter, but also so that we can get to work on time.

"It would have been a better morning if you would have wakened me the way you used to instead of sending our daughter to do your dirty work," I say with my voice sounding as aroused as I feel.

"Oh please, that never got you out of bed before. If anything we'd both be late because we'd still be up there right now."

"That's precisely my point," I say as I playfully pat her round bottom. "You know you've been too busy to take care of me lately," I say with mock sadness.

Janice shoots me a sharp glance. "Ryan Du Bois, you lie like you breathe. You know full well, I always take care of you. It's not my fault you're insatiable."

I take my seat at the breakfast table as Janice places a plate of food in front of me. "Actually dear, it is your fault. How could I live with you and not be turned on every day?"

Janice turns to look at me and playfully lifts the front of her skirt as she speaks, "Go to work and handle all of the boring stuff today and tonight the fun stuff will be right here waiting." Janice pats the front of her pink lace panties before putting her skirt back down and turning to walk out of the kitchen. I know she is going to get Kaitlin so I will my member to calm down. I've always been an extremely disciplined man, but my wife pushes me to the edge. If I can remain this attracted to her for the rest of our lives I will die a very happy man.

A few moments later Janice re-enters the kitchen with a not so happy Kaitlin in tow. "What's the matter with Daddy's princess?" I ask my teary daughter.

"Kaitlin see Bubble Guppies."

"It's okay sweetie, Bubble Guppies will be there after you eat. Why don't you sit here and eat with Daddy?"

Kaitlin doesn't seem happy but she doesn't fuss when Janice lowers her into her seat next to me. Janice joins us and I quickly say grace before we all dig into the pancakes and sausage Janice prepared. Most families only eat dinner together, but Janice and I decided we'd enjoy breakfast together as often as possible as well. There are times when I have to go into work early or work late to prepare for cases I receive at the last minute, but for the most part I spend my mornings and evenings with the two people that motivate me to continue my job.

After breakfast Janice clears the table while I say goodbye to Kaitlin. It is a chore to say goodbye to her in the mornings. She doesn't cry when I leave for work, but she makes sure I know she's not happy about it. Today is no different. It took a full two minutes to redirect her focus back to the lifesaving Bubble Guppies. I return to the kitchen to kiss Janice goodbye. She's waiting for me with a naughty smile on her face. She doesn't have to say a word. As soon as I see her I know what she has in mind. I glance over my shoulder communicating my question about our daughter. Janice smiles.

"If you're quick counselor, she won't even know we're missing."

I smile as my wife pulls me into the guest bedroom located just off of the kitchen. Janice wastes no time making sure I'm taken care of before leaving for work. If I did not appreciate her before this morning, I definitely appreciate her now. She's perfect for me in every way.

***

I enter the office at exactly 7:30 am. I technically do not have a scheduled report time, though we all usually arrive around 7. I decide I must have picked the wrong morning to take thirty extra minutes when I see my boss Thomas Willoughby walking out of my office. I steel myself in anticipation of a reprimand, when Thomas surprises me by smiling.

"Ryan, hey glad I could catch you before I headed to court. Do you have a minute?"

I play it cool even though it is anything but ordinary for Thomas to even speak to me, let alone ask me if I have a minute for him. A simple "sure" is all I can muster out as I continue into my office. Thomas turns and follows me back inside. He closes the door behind him, yet another thing I find odd.

I place my briefcase on my desk and remain standing. I nervously stuff both hands into my pockets. Something is not right here, but I'm not sure if Thomas will tell me exactly what it is. I try the indirect approach. "What can I do for you boss?"

"Please, take your seat," Thomas insists a little too pleasantly.

I furrow my brow unable to hide my confusion. Instead of asking another question I oblige and take my seat behind my desk. Thomas sits in one of the two chairs facing me. He looks nervous. I try to recall the last time I've seen him nervous. My mind draws a blank. It's never happened. I wait with anticipation building for Thomas to say something, anything to let me know why he is behaving so weirdly. Just when I think I can no longer handle the anticipation, Thomas begins to speak.

"Ryan, your work here has been exemplary."

I listen and mentally moan as I know this is the type of compliment one gets before being thrown to the wolves. I keep my facial expression stoic in hopes he cannot tell how much I am dreading the remainder of this conversation.

"I've noticed for quite some time that you really seem to have a heart for the innocent."

I find it odd that he'd notice anything about me since he mostly ignores my presence but again I remain quiet while he continues to speak.

"I just received a call about a case that I want to personally ask you to handle. It's a unique case that will draw quite a bit of controversy, but for reasons I can't disclose I can't personally defend this client. I will be assigning the case to you today, but wanted to speak with you directly before the announcement is made to the rest of the team."

I want to gasp, but I do my best to keep my expression even. A high profile case will be just what I need to quit this awful job and move forward with the plan Janice and I have been working on. I keep my voice steady as I ask, "Can I ask which case you are referring to?"

"Like I said, it's a new case," Thomas stammers. "The client is a father of four that was arrested for killing his infant daughter."

This time I do not succeed in holding my gasp inside. A murder? Thomas wants me to defend someone on a murder charge. Has this man lost his mind? The biggest case I've ever been assigned to involved a prostitution ring. How in the hell was I supposed to defend a murder suspect?

"Thomas, I'm flattered, but I'm not sure I'm the best attorney for this case. I've never even dealt with any misdemeanors involving violence and now you want me to take on a murder charge? And he killed a child? I have a daughter Thomas. I'd die before I hurt her. I can't defend a man that killed his own child."

Thomas' face hardens. Here comes the Thomas I know and loathe. "You know the rules of this office. We defend the clients we're given. We can't pick and choose. You've been here long enough to know we have to check the personal bullshit at the door and give each client the defense they deserve. Now if you've decided you can no longer do that, you know where to find the door. You have about 30 minutes to decide. If you come to the morning meeting prepared to be briefed on your case I'll assume you've worked out your bias. If not, I'll assume you've quit."

I hang my head feeling the weight of the case already. I feel like there's an anvil hanging around my neck and I haven't even viewed the case file or interviewed the client. None of this makes any sense. Why is Thomas throwing this at me now? What's really going on?

"Thomas, can I be frank with you?"

"By all means, please do."

"Why me? You and I both know you barely even speak to me. Why am I suddenly your go to guy?"

Thomas is obviously taken aback by the question, but he wastes no time answering. "You're right. Ordinarily this case would have gone to Kate, but in case you forgot she no longer works here. Now the rest of you are going to have to do more than petty larceny cases."

Thomas stands up and walks out of my office without so much as a glance in my direction signaling the end of our conversation. I may be a young man, but I'm not a dumb one. I've just been set up and I'm not sure why.

Chapter 2
Ryan

I pop two aspirin and force them down with water
before exiting my blue metallic CLA45 Coupe.
Ordinarily riding in the one thing I actually splurge on
brought me a sense of peace, but after this morning's
impromptu ambush by Thomas nothing seems to be
able to calm my nerves. Hence my splitting headache. I
pray the aspirin begin to work their magic quickly as I
have to meet with my baby killing client in just a few
minutes. The county jail is always an interesting place
to visit. There are all sorts of characters from hardened
criminals who are denied bail to the wide range of
characters that work to keep the inmates in line. I take
a long deep breath unsure of what I am about to
encounter. As much as I hate to admit it, Thomas has a
point about my caring for the client. I don't like finding

out about people that wrongfully spent years of their lives behind bars because of inadequate counsel. I can't imagine a reason a father would actually murder his own flesh and blood. I think of my own daughter. Kaitlin is the purest parts of her mother and me. I would never do anything to hurt her. I have to believe most fathers would agree with me. There has to be some sort of mistake or explanation. From what I could gather in my quick perusal of the file, Evan Reynolds has no record of abuse claims or any prior run-ins with the law. Two of his older children are in college and the third is a high school student. It seems odd that he and his wife decided to have another baby after so many years but not completely out of the ordinary. It's not uncommon for parents fearing the impending empty nest to have another child or for a woman to become pregnant during the pre-menopausal years. Still, I file the information away for later thought.

I enter the jail and head straight to the check in area. One of my favorite deputies is manning the visitor's desk today. He smiles when he looks up and sees me approaching.

"Hey Ry-man, what's goin on?"

Harvey insists on calling me Ry which he often follows up with the word man. I'm still not sure how I became *Ry-man*, a nickname I loathe because of how similar it is to Rain-man, but I reply all the same. "Hi Harvey. You know how it is, same shit just a different toilet."

Harvey laughs a little too loudly. "That's why I like you Ry-man. You're the funniest lawyer I've ever met, especially for a white dude."

Though I like Harvey, he always seems to say something racially inappropriate. I could end the jokes by pointing out the fact that I'm actually a New Orleans bred man born to a Caucasian father and fair skinned African American mother, but that would start a whole conversation I don't have time for so I play along. I grab my chest and pretend to be insulted. "For a white dude? I thought I was all around funny! Not just white dude funny!"

"You know what? You the man hands down!"

I chuckle and continue the small talk with Harvey while he checks me into the system. After he gives me the necessary visitor credentials I make my way down the long corridor leading to the private visiting rooms. My conversations with my clients are confidential so we are allowed a little time away from the listening ears around us to discuss the case. Normally I enter the room and have an opportunity to review my files one last time before the client is brought in to meet with me. Today however, I enter the room to find Evan Reynolds already waiting for me. Evan is not what I expect. With the exception of his hair which could stand a decent trim, he looks a lot like me. He's shaven and tanned with clear skin and hands that look like he hasn't done a hard day's work in his life. He looks up at me and I realize that's where our similarities end. Evan's eyes are dark. I stare directly into them and see nothing. There's no remorse, no fear, no anger...no emotion whatsoever. My first thought is this guy is a complete sociopath as I feel anger rise within me. What kind of monster drowns his own baby? I close my eyes and take a deep breath before I walk over to the table and take the seat in front of him. Regardless of what he's done, he's entitled to a fair trial. It's my job to make sure he receives one, even though I want to choke the shit out of him right here in the visitor's room.

"Mr. Reynolds, my name is Ryan Du Bois and I have been assigned as your attorney for the purposes of this trial. We only have a day to prepare for your bail hearing so we need to go over the facts as quickly as possible."

"I don't want bail."

"Excuse me?"

"I don't want bail. I deserve to rot in here for what happened to my little girl."

"Mr. Reynolds, if you believe that, why did you request a lawyer?"

"Because I didn't kill her."

"I'm confused. You just said you deserve to rot in here for what you did."

"No I didn't," Evan said a little louder than expected. "I said I deserve to rot in here for what happened to her. My little girl drowned. I was the only one in the house when it happened, but I don't remember anything. I swear," he continued as tears began to pool in his eyes. "I swear I would never do anything to hurt my baby. I love all of my children more than life itself but my baby girl is dead and I can't remember anything. I don't even remember getting out of bed that day."

"Tell me what you do remember," I say to Evan as I reach into my briefcase and pull out a pen and notepad. I didn't expect to have to take notes during this meeting but after what my client just revealed I realize I have no clue what I've just walked into.

"I remember arguing with Lisa the night before. She's been nagging me about my drinking and staying out too late for months, but that night she accused me of having an affair. She was yelling about wanting a divorce and threatening to take my kids away from me."

"What did you say?"

"That's just it. My head was killing me and her yelling was making it worse so I didn't say anything. I remember taking a couple aspirin and hopping in the shower. When I got out of the shower Lisa was sitting on the side of the bed crying. I can't stand to see her cry. Even after all of these years we've been married a piece of me still breaks when she's hurting. I tried to comfort her and assure her I could never cheat on her, but she just blew up on me again and stormed out of the room. My head was hurting so bad I didn't have the energy to chase after her so I just went to bed. I was hoping I could just sleep the headache off."

"How long have you been suffering from these headaches?"

"They started a few months ago but they were mild. They just started getting real intense a couple weeks ago."

"Have you seen a doctor?"

Evan looks up at me as though I've insulted him to his core.

"A doctor?" he questions with a hint of surprise in his voice. "Who goes to the doctor for a headache?"

"What you're describing sounds worse than a simple headache," I say in a serious tone. "From what you're telling me, your headaches are becoming progressively worse and may even be accompanied by black outs. This could be serious."

I stand and begin stuffing the notepad back into my briefcase.

"That's it?" Evan questions.

"Yes. That's it for now. I need to get you examined by a doctor as soon as possible. I think you may be very seriously ill."

Chapter 3
Michael

I roll over and watch my wife as she sleeps. The sun is just starting to sneak into the room, but even in the dimness I can see she's still the most beautiful woman I've ever seen. I take a moment to appreciate her. The rise and fall of her chest are mesmerizing, especially coupled with her swollen belly that's carrying our first child. I reach out and lay my hand on her belly. As always my son responds to my touch with a strong kick. My wife stirs. Her eyes flutter open and I see I've angered her yet again.

"Dammit Michael, why can't you wait for me to wake up before you wake him?"

Kate turns away from me exposing her round hips and ass. I stare at her curves and feel my erection awakening. I know I should keep my hands to myself but, somewhere deep down inside of me, I believe she does this on purpose. She knows how her body turns me on, yet she seems to always turn her back to me... teasing me, beckoning me to move closer which will surely be too much for me to resist.

I slide behind my wife, wrapping my arm around her and ending up in her favorite position, the spoon. She wriggles her hips as she settles into me, a move she knows will send me over the edge. My erection leaps involuntarily and presses into her bottom.

"Really Michael?" Kate tries to sound annoyed, but I know better. Now that she's in her second trimester, her sex drive is through the roof and that little wriggle she does is her sure fire "come and get it" move.

"It's not my fault. You know how he gets when you push yourself into him like that."

Kate giggles before starting to get out of the bed. I lock my arms around her preventing her from leaving the warmth of our bed. "Wait, you can't leave me here like this," I say gently pushing my erection against her.

"Your son is tap dancing on my bladder. Give me five minutes to relieve myself and freshen up."

I reluctantly release her and watch as she walks slowly into the bathroom. As she closes the door behind her my cell phone rings. I seriously consider ignoring it, but know the caller will more than likely keep calling if I don't answer. I decide it's best to handle the call quickly before Kate comes back to bed.

"This is Michael."

"Michael, this is Ron Edahl. There's been an accident."

"What kind of accident?"

"One that involves police."

I jolt upright. "Have you said anything to them?"

"No. They're not here yet, but it's a matter of minutes at this point."

I hop out of bed and begin franticly looking for my clothes. "Where are you?"

"I'm at home."

"Good. Don't open the door for them when they get there. Tell them through the door that your lawyer is on the way. Don't say anything else. No matter what they say and do not open that door!"

"But Michael..."

"No buts Ron. Don't open your mouth, except to tell them I'm coming. I'll be there in less than ten minutes."

"But Michael there's something you should know."

The tone in his voice halts me. It's empty yet taunting...like something inside of him is dying to get out. The silence is thick as I wait for him to say the words. I hear him clear his throat before a small sob escapes him, followed by many more just like it. I sit down at the foot of my bed as my wife reappears from the bathroom, worry creeps onto her face as soon as she sees me. Then I hear a break in the sobs, followed by Ron's voice which is now extremely weak.

"Michelle is dead. I killed her."

***

The short drive to Ron's house is a blur. I've known
Ron and his wife Patty for as long as I can remember.
They were like second parents to me as a kid, giving me
what little morals I possess. They were our next door
neighbors up until my 12th birthday. I spent many
nights at their dinner table long before they had a child
of their own. Ron and I haven't remained as close over
the years, but I've always seen him as a cross between a
really cool big brother and a back-up dad. He and Patty
were there for all of the major events in my life, every
graduation, my award ceremony where the Mayor
honored me for my role in taking down the former
chief of police, and my wedding. He's always been a
gentle and patient soul. Even though I heard him say
the words, I can't imagine him hurting anyone...much
less his only child.

Ron and Patty suffered from fertility issues. It's part of
the reason they spent so much time with me when I
was young. They desperately wanted to fill their home
with the laughter of children, but every fertility
treatment they tried failed. When Patty finally got
pregnant with Michelle, everyone was so excited. They
were older first time parents than most, but they were

over the moon with joy. Finally having their prayers answered made both of them beam with excitement. They turned all the years of heartache into love and poured it into Michelle. The child's every request was granted from the time she could talk. It made Ron and Patty happy when their yeses put a smile on their miracle baby's face. As often seen in cases like this, the focus on loving their miracle clouded their judgment in key areas. Neither parent gave Michelle the discipline she needed. She was a headache to both Ron and Patty since her pre-teen years. It was mostly typical rebellious behavior until she started hanging out with some kids she met online. That's when Ron called me in to help.

Michelle's first bout with legal trouble began six months ago with underage drinking. She was subsequently kicked out of Charlotte Country Day School, a prestigious private school that is as exclusive as it is expensive. For her second act, she attempted to steal from a jewelry store in South Park Mall, the city's most impressive shopping hotspot. Since she'd only been attending her court mandated therapy sessions for a few weeks, I was able to convince a judge that community service would be a better sentence rather than putting her in juvenile detention where her therapy would be interrupted. Neither therapy nor community service were serious enough deterrents because just last week Patty found a small bag of pills in Michelle's bedroom. The pair argued before Michelle threw a few items into a bag and stormed out of the house. Patty called me in tears, afraid Michelle would miss her therapy and community service appointments. My calls to Michelle went unanswered. Yet, the following day when I went to her therapist's office, there she was...sitting in the waiting room reading a magazine as though nothing happened. When asked why she decided to show up for therapy after running away from home, her reply was simple. She didn't want to go to jail. I had to admit she was reckless, but smart.

I pull into Ron and Patty's driveway forcing my thoughts back to present day. I've never been more thankful for the location of Ron's home. Being so far outside of the city limits and being in such a quiet, remote area means the police take forever to arrive after they've been called. I'm still a little shocked I've beat them here, but this works to our advantage. I want to get inside and assess the scene before the police do.

I need to quickly learn as much as possible to advise Ron on how to respond to their questions. Ron opens the front door before I can even exit the car. He rushes out, mouth open prepared to speak but I hold up my hand in protest.

"No! Don't say a word out here. I know you can't see your neighbors, but we can't take any chances. Let's go inside."

Ron turns and goes back up the stairs with me on his heels. Once inside, I close the door behind me and get right to business.

"What happened?"

"I thought he was hurting her. I lost it. Then I felt something hit me in the back of the head. I didn't look to see who it was. I acted on impulse. I didn't realize it was Michelle until after she fell. She hit her head. Michael...." Ron burst into tears again.

I hear the faint sounds of sirens. I touch Ron's arm. "Show me where she is."

Though he never stops sobbing, Ron turns and starts walking. I follow him. When he stops in the open doorway of a room I assume to be Michelle's bedroom, he falls to his knees and doubles over in tears. I hear the faint cries of a female and assume it's Patty. I step around Ron and peer into the room. My hand instantly goes to my mouth. The scene before me is one of the most gruesome I've ever seen. At the foot of the bed lay the body of a man whose face has been beaten beyond recognition. I can tell that he is a black man with long dreadlocks and a tattoo of praying hands on the left side of his chest. He's laying naked in a pool of his own blood.

I quickly scan the rest of the room. Near the nightstand next to the head of the bed lay a body covered in a sheet. I assume this is Michelle. I walk over and stop short of the blood pooled around the top of the body. I make sure not to step in the blood as I lean down and lift the sheet. Michelle's face is the perfect picture of peace. If not for the blood, Patty crying in the corner, Ron crying at the door, and the other dead body in the room I would have assumed the girl was sleeping.

The sounds of the sirens grow closer as I spring into action. I corral a resistant Patty out of the room and over to Ron.

"Ron, you didn't tell me there was someone else here. What happened?"

"We were awakened by screams. We attended the Cure for Lupus Benefit Gala last night and got in very late. We hadn't seen Michelle since she stormed out. I normally check her room when we come home. I always hope she'll be here but I didn't last night. I was just too exhausted." Patty said through tears. "Then the screams woke us up. We thought she was in trouble. Ron jumped out of bed and raced in here. I followed as quickly as I could, but by the time I got to the room Ron was on top of the young man beating him senseless. I yelled for Ron to stop. I tried to pull him off of him, but Ron was crazed. He pushed me away and just kept punching and punching him. Michelle was screaming for Ron to stop...something about her being in love with him. And then it hit me. Michelle had been bragging about her new boyfriend and how he was going to free her from us. I tried telling Ron, but nothing was coming out right. It was all happening so fast. Then Michelle picked up that lamp," Patty's speech slowed as she pointed to the broken lamp on the floor. "She hit Ron on the back of the head with it and he swung backwards. I don't think Michelle was expecting the hit because she didn't brace herself. She couldn't have. There was no time. He just hit her and she flew backwards. I saw the nightstand, knew she was going to hit it, but I couldn't get to her in time to catch her. As soon as her head hit the corner blood sprayed everywhere and I knew it was too late."

I glance over in the direction of Michelle's lifeless body once more and spot the blood on the corner of the nightstand. It was an accident. Ron had killed his only child, the child he and his wife spent the bulk of their life praying for. It was an accident. One he'd likely never recover from, one neither of them would recover from. Yet, I could spare him prison time. The major problem lay with the second body. Ron beat a man to death with his bare hands. A thought occurs to me as I hear the first knock at the front door. I hear the police announce themselves, but I still turn to ask Patty the question.

"Patty, do you know how old Michelle's boyfriend is...was?" I stutter.

"No. I don't think she ever told me."

"Think Patty. This is very important. Did she say anything that could give away his age? Anything at all?" I urge Patty as the police knocks grow more intense.

Patty's hand rushes to her mouth as her eyes grow wide with realization. "Oh my God," she mutters. "He's just a child. He's a senior at her new school. He plays football. That's why Michelle said he was going to take her away. She said he was going to be an NFL star. Oh my God Ron! You killed a child!"

Chapter 4
Ryan

"What do you mean I shouldn't request bail? We always request bail," I say in frustration as I stare at my boss.

"In the past we have requested bail. I'm telling you not to on this one," Thomas says with a don't-you-dare-challenge-me look on his face.

I ignore the expression. "If I don't request bail, it'll look like I'm not even trying. What happened to you wanting to make sure we give all clients the best defense possible?"

Thomas narrows his eyes as he glares at me. "Since once again you spoke before you actually thought, I'll break it down for you. Your client is currently in jail for drowning his infant daughter. You think he's suffering from some sort of neurological issue that is causing him headaches and blackouts because for some reason unbeknownst to me, you believe him when he says he doesn't remember anything from the morning his daughter died. You want to get him released so that he can be seen by a doctor. Is all of this correct so far?"

I nod by head but I don't bother to try to hide the frustration on my face.

"Have you ever stopped to consider that having the State provide his medical care would be irrefutable proof of your theory? That is...if he's actually ill as you suggest?"

It finally clicks. Thomas is telling me to leave Evan in prison so that the prosecutor won't be able to refute the medical findings. I smile sheepishly.

"You can thank me later. For now, get your arrogant ass out of my office. And don't insult me or my commitment to this office ever again," Thomas booms.

I stand without a word feeling like a fool once again. This always happens when I challenge Thomas. The man is like the Nostradamus of legal theory. One would think all of his underlings, myself included, would know better than to challenge him, yet we do...often. As I reach the door I hear Thomas call my name. I stop and turn to face him.

"It's later," he says without the tiniest hint of a smile.

"Thanks," I mumble in irritation as I head back to my own office.

I grab the receiver of my phone and begin dialing before I can even take my seat. It takes less than two minutes for me to speak to the powers that be over at the county lockup. I describe Evan's symptoms and explain he needs to be seen by a doctor immediately. I hear a laugh at the other end of the phone. I pull the phone away from my ear and look at it. I feel my anger boiling just beneath the surface.

"You're laughing at my request for my client to be seen by a doctor?" I shout as loud as I possibly can, hoping to hurt the prick's ear.

"Look, this is jail, not day care. We aren't sending anyone to a hospital unless it's absolutely necessary, a real medical emergency. A headache is not an emergency. Good bye."

I stare at the phone with incredulity. I can't believe he hung up on me. I can't even believe he laughed at me. I stand once again and grab my jacket from the back of my chair. I storm out of the office knowing full well I shouldn't do what I am about to do. I'm going to do it anyway.

***

"You want me to fake a blackout?" Evan asks as he stares at me in confusion.

"Lower your voice!" I admonish him. "I'm not telling you to fake anything. I'm telling you to make sure the guards are aware of your headaches. Do not suffer in silence, and don't give them any reason not to believe you are losing chunks of your day. I'll handle everything on my end. You just be as little help to them as possible."

Evan closes his eyes and tilts his head back slightly. I'm not quite sure what he's doing so I just sit there watching him quietly. After a long pause he looks at me and says, "I really do need something for this headache."

I can't tell if he's trying to play the part I just instructed him to play or if he's really in pain, which is exactly what I want. "I'll make a formal request for you to receive medical care as quickly as possible," I say as I stand and prepare to leave.

"Do you think you could do one more thing for me?"

I stop moving and give Evan my full attention. "Sure, what do you need?"

"I haven't spoken to my wife Lisa since...." his voice trails off as his eyes start to fill with tears. He closes his eyes as a single tear rolls from each eye. He takes a moment to regain his composure. "Can you speak with my wife and see if she'll be willing to come visit me?"

I nod. "Sure Evan. I'll speak with Lisa."

***

My original intention was to return to the office after meeting with Evan, but seeing and hearing his sadness tugged at my heart. I pull his file from my briefcase and search for his home address. Within minutes I'm on my way to his home in east Charlotte. The only thing I know about the area is what I've seen on the news, so I don't like the idea of going over there so late in the day. Janice will kill me if she finds out, but I figure talking with Mrs. Reynolds should not take very long, especially since I am showing up unannounced.

I pull up to the small brick duplex and park behind a blue, older model Toyota Camry. I quickly exit hoping the car means Lisa Reynolds is at home. This neighborhood is not exactly known for welcoming strangers. A strange man in a suit driving an expensive car stands out like a hooker in church. I knock on the door and take a small step backward waiting for Lisa to respond. After a few seconds I step forward and knock again. I hear a female's voice respond from the inside.

"Who is it?"

"It's Ryan Du Bois. I'm the attorney assigned to Evan's case."

I stand there listening to my heart pound in my chest, realizing my anxiety level is much higher than I thought it would be. Meeting with Evan's wife should be simple, but judging by the way I'm currently feeling and the fact that the woman on the other side of the door just lost her daughter, I'm guessing simplicity isn't an option. I hear movement inside the house and see someone peek out of the window. I smile even though my stomach feels as though it is going to betray me at any moment. I listen as locks are turned and watch the door swing open to reveal a beautiful petite dark skinned woman dressed in nursing scrubs. I notice she is black, a fact Evan didn't mention, but then again why should he? I make a mental note about the potential race related issues that could arise during the course of this case. Given the current state of race relations in Charlotte, a white man acquitted of the murder of his infant mixed race daughter could cause quite a stir, especially within the black community. Last year I was publicly accused of not doing enough to help a young black man beat a robbery conviction, once again my mixed race heritage was ignored due to the fairness of my skin. I do my best not to let my personal feelings interfere with the way I handle cases, so I push the thoughts back out of my mind and focus on the woman standing in front of me.

"Are you Lisa Reynolds?" I ask the question even though I already know the answer. Her round eyes are red and swollen, classic signs of a person who has been crying.

"Yes," she responds in a clear strong voice, much stronger than I expected.

"Do you think it would be possible for me to come in and speak with you about your husband's case?"

Lisa folds her arms and looks at me defiantly. "No it would not be possible for you to come inside and speak to me about anything. You have approximately five minutes to say your peace and get off my property before I call the police."

Her tight face and posture leave no doubt in my mind about the truthfulness of her words. I jump right in before I run out of time. "Mrs. Reynolds, your husband asked me to come speak to you. He wants to know if you'll come visit him."

"You tell that son of a bitch it'll be a cold day in hell before I come anywhere near him. The only time he'll see my face is when I get on the stand to tell everyone how he chose drinking over the safety of my baby."

"Evan says he wasn't drinking."

"Evan is a bold face liar. He was drunk as shit that morning. I could barely get him out of the bed."

"And you just left your daughter with a drunk man?"

Lisa took a step towards me and unfolded her arms placing them firmly on her hips, a clear sign I was in trouble. "What the hell are you trying to say?"

I hold my hands up hoping she'll see the sign of surrender and calm down. "I'm not trying to say anything other than if you truly believed Evan was drunk you wouldn't have left your daughter with him."

"You don't know what I would do. You don't know shit about me or Evan. How dare you bring your sorry ass around here making assumptions about what I would or wouldn't do! I'm a damn good mother," she says, closing the distance between us and waving her finger up towards my face. "I've held this family together for years while your client pissed his life and career away in the bottom of a bottle!"

I take a small step backward. "I apologize," I say in a softer tone hoping she'll follow suit and calm down a little. "Look, I didn't mean to get on your bad side by making assumptions. I'm only trying to investigate so that I can properly defend your husband."

"Don't you call him that," she hisses.

"Again, I apologize. I'm trying to defend Evan. Based on what he's told me, I fear he may be very ill. I only wanted to deliver his request to see you and ask you a few questions about his health and behavior prior to the incident."

As soon as the words leave my mouth I know I've made a grave mistake. Lisa Reynolds tears into me with a slew of insults and profanity that would make a sailor blush. I quickly begin retreating to my car as it is apparent the conversation is past the point of salvation. As I get into my car and close the door I notice Lisa is standing in front of my car. I didn't even know she was behind me. I start the engine within seconds of her banging on my hood. I haul ass out of her driveway and down the street, with one thought in mind. If Lisa Reynolds is this crazy, what does that say about her husband?

Chapter 5
Michael

I loosen my tie as I walk into my office. I head straight for the mini fridge and grab a bottle of water. I desperately want something stronger, but Kate has banned all alcohol from the office. No matter how many times I sneak a bottle of Scotch in, she always manages to get rid of it before I can even crack it open. I swear the woman must have some sort of alcohol detector in her brain.

I plop down in my chair and curse under my breath. The last few days since finding out Ron murdered two children in cold blood have been a total blur for me. So far, I have managed to save my client from experiencing the humiliation and shame of county lockup. I know how terrible even a second behind bars can be, and I was in jail less than an hour. It would be devastating for Ron who is grieving the loss of his only child. I've also kept the story from hitting the news. I know I won't be able to keep the vultures at bay for long, but at least Patty and Ron will be able to lay their daughter to rest today without the media videotaping their every move. I take a long swig of water from my bottle and replay Ron's statement to the police in my mind. We told them about Ron and Patty both believing Michelle was being attacked. We told them about Michelle startling Ron with the lamp and his subsequent swing that sent her flying backwards into the night stand. I encouraged Ron to show as much emotion as he could, remorse would be a key factor. I'd hoped we would be able to avoid charges, but my old nemesis Bart Winslow is the DA's number one prosecutor, so there is no chance he'll miss an opportunity to stick it to me. After the way I humiliated him during his last attempt to prosecute one of my clients, a 16 year old girl charged with murder, Bart has been trying to get back at me. Once again I fear a client may suffer because of Bart's personal vendetta against me. I know I need to file a grievance with the North

Carolina State Bar Association to put an end to Bart's harassment, but our previous friendship won't let me. No matter how much he hates me, there is still a part of me that misses the fun loving guy I grew up with. For years, Bart was the closest thing I had to a brother, but the death of his mother turned him into someone I barely recognize. My father's disgracing of his father, and my subsequently taking over the firm our fathers built from the ground up, only thickened Bart's hate for me.

On the positive side of my current legal dilemma, Ron and I gave a solid factual statement. On the other hand, we omitted the fact that Michelle and the young man were dating. As far as I can tell, there is no way for the police to discover that Michelle actually told her mother about the relationship. I realize it is a lie of omission, but it is a fact that could seriously hurt Ron, a good man that lost his temper in the heat of the moment. Burying his daughter will be punishment for a lifetime.

My wife Kate disagrees with my decision to withhold that information. Good ole Kate, the center of my moral compass. She urged me to allow Ron to tell the whole truth. I decided it was a risk we simply could not afford to take. Kate has rewarded my decision by not speaking to me. I'm not sure if it's pregnancy hormones or a general distaste for the way I handle cases, but she seems to be spending more and more time disagreeing with me at work. In the year that has passed since we started working together, Kate has spent more time not talking to me than she has actually talking to me. The fact that we actually communicated enough to get pregnant is astonishing. Although it shouldn't be. Kate spends her time pissed at me. My heart still skips a beat when she walks into a room. She's given me more than anyone ever has and that fact alone keeps me calm even when I want to be angry.

"Come in," I yell in response to the knock on my door.

I look up to see Tanya entering my office. Tanya has worked for Kate and I since I returned to work after being shot. She's still as flirty as she was when we worked together in the Public Defender's office, but she's much more demure and professional. She eyes me like she always does, like I am the last biscuit the world will ever see, as she takes the seat across from me.

"Good morning Boss," she purrs in a tone I know and loathe.

"Good morning Tanya. What can I do for you?"

"Well, I want to thank you for giving me the opportunity to work for you, but I'm afraid I'm going to have to resign."

"And why is that?"

"Thomas has offered me my old job back with a sizeable pay raise."

Thomas is our old boss over at the Public Defender's office. He's a wise and fair man, but he spends most of his time making everyone around him feel small. He hasn't been happy with me since I stole Kate and Tanya away from him. I'm not surprised he's trying to take Tanya back. Although rough around the edges, she's grown to be a very capable legal secretary which is the only reason I put up any sort of resistance to her leaving.

"So you'd rather go back to that dust bowl where you were overlooked for years than stay here and continue to grow in your profession?"

Tanya smiles. "I appreciate everything you and Kate have done for me, but the bottom line is I could use the money. I'm trying to buy a house and the increase in pay is going to look really nice on my loan application."

I lean forward and rest my elbows on my desk. "So this is purely a pay issue? Nothing else?"

"That's right."

I lean back again. "That's an easy fix. I'll retro a twenty percent pay raise back to the beginning of the quarter. Tell Thomas you'll be staying right here."

"Thank you Michael! Twenty percent is way more than I expected!" Tanya exclaims as she leaps from her seat and heads towards the door.

"Tanya," I call out, stopping her in her tracks. She turns to face me.

"You and I both know Thomas called you but he didn't offer you a raise. He can't arbitrarily increase a state employee's salary. In the future, if you need more money, just ask. You don't have to lie to me."

Tanya smiles and places her large hand on her ample hip. "In that case, can I ask you for..."

I hold up my hand cutting her off. "No ma'am, you're not getting anything else out of me for the rest of the year. Now get back to work before I change my mind about the raise."

Tanya's smile stays plastered on her face as she turns and attempts to sashay out of the office. I shudder at the sight of such a masculine looking woman attempting to be flirty before I look away. Judging by all the flowers that get delivered for her, plenty of men find Tanya attractive, I on the other hand, will stick with Kate, my tennis playing, perfectly feminine wife.

I glance at my watch and realize I only have half an hour to get across town for Michelle's memorial service. I stand and grab my jacket before heading out the door. I stop when I see a familiar face standing in the reception area. A smile quickly spreads across my face as I rush over to her.

"Nadine! What in the world are you doing here?" I ask as I wrap my arms around her and pull her in for a hug. Nadine and I bonded over my former client, Shamika Carrington, and have remained close ever since. She was and still remains more of a mother to me than my own mother will ever be.

"Well, I was over at the mall picking up a few things and decided to drop by. I haven't spoken to you in weeks, so I figured I come deliver your tongue lashing in person."

My smile fades slightly, just enough to show her I am genuinely apologetic. "I'm sorry Nadine. You know I'd never ignore you intentionally. I've just been swamped here at the office and I got another really big case a few days ago. I'm actually heading out to be with my client now. You barely caught me."

"I know. Kate told me all about it. It's a shame what he did to those poor children."

My smile vanishes completely. "Kate talked to you about my case?"

"Yes," Nadine says in a tone that dares me to chastise her. "I couldn't reach you so I called Kate and she mentioned it."

I move away from Nadine and step towards the elevators. "I'm sorry Nadine, but I really do have to get going. I can't be late." I push the call button on the wall and step back as I wait for the elevator. Nadine walks up beside me.

"Look Michael, I know this isn't any of my business..."

"Then stay out of it Nadine," I say a little more harshly than I intend. My tone pushes Nadine over the edge and her fiery side comes rushing out.

"Now you look here Michael Ayers, in case you forgot I'm not one of these simpletons you can push around. I came here out of concern for you and your marriage, but if you want to act like an ass I'll leave you right where I found you. And don't come crawling to me later asking for advice because I won't be handing any out."

With that she turns and walks away from me. I watch her go in the direction of Kate's office but I don't have time to follow behind her. The elevator arrives and I step inside totally perplexed about her statement. Sure things have been tense between Kate and I recently, but our marriage isn't in trouble. Is it?

Chapter 6
Michael

I arrive at Michelle's memorial service with less than a minute to spare and instantly begin to feel sick. The entrance to the church parking lot is lined with news vans. How the hell did they find out about Michelle and the memorial? I turn into the parking lot as cameras flash from every direction. I begin to physically feel sick as I think of how terrible Ron and Patty must be feeling to have their only daughter's memorial service crashed by reporters. I pull into a parking space, exit my vehicle and forcefully push my way through the throng of reporters that surrounded my car as soon as it stopped. I fight the urge to throw punches while cursing them all as I make my way up the steps and into the church. I glance around the room looking for my client but all I see are red faced teenagers. Despite what Michelle may have led everyone to believe, she was very popular and well liked. The large turnout of teenagers I'm currently looking at is proof Michelle was the sweet loving girl Patty and Ron believed her to be.

I look to my left after feeling someone tug on my arm. It's Patty's sister Susan. I reach out and give her a warm hug trying to offer her what little strength I have to spare. She clings to me obviously needing the moment. When she pulls back I notice her face is wet with tears. I dig into my pocket and retrieve one of the handkerchiefs my mother always insisted I carry as a young teen. I hated it then, but as a man I realize the wisdom of her teaching. I hand the handkerchief to Susan who accepts it and dabs at her face.

"I was supposed to be bringing you to the back to see Ron and Patty, but your hug distracted me. I've been trying to be so strong for Patty that I didn't realize how much I needed a simple hug. Thanks for that."

"Don't mention it. This is an impossibly difficult situation. Where are Ron and Patty?"

"Follow me."

She turns and heads down a side aisle. I follow her feeling the eyes of hundreds of young people watch me with more scrutiny than I'm comfortable with. I've made countless speeches and arguments in front of juries and camera crews have been in my face more than most, and I've never been more nervous. All the sad eyes on me make my own emotions threaten to betray me. I swallow hard as I enter the side door closing it behind me. Both Ron and Patty are sitting at a small table sobbing. I stand silent for a moment not wanting to interrupt them. A tear leaks from my eye before I can stop it. Watching the two of them grieve into each other is more than I can stand. Between them there is more love for children than I've ever witnessed, yet here they sit grieving the death of their miracle baby. Ron showed me the love of a father, now circumstances have led to him taking the life of not only an innocent young boy, but his own flesh and blood as well. I subconsciously pull on my tie struggling to breathe. I feel a panic attack coming on. I turn to leave the room, but Ron calls out to me.

"No Michael, don't leave."

I stop and turn back to face him struggling to hold my liquid emotions inside. I fail as large tears begin pouring down my face. Ron stands and embraces me in the tightest hug I've ever received from a man. I hate myself for allowing him to comfort me when it should be the other way around. I don't pull away though. I selfishly allow him to share what little strength he has left with me until I feel I'm strong enough to make it through the funeral. I pull back and place my hand on his shoulders.

"I'm sorry I fell apart. I should be the one comforting you," I say as I look into his tear swollen eyes.

"Nonsense Michael. Michelle was the closest you'll ever come to having a sibling. Hell, we even named her after you," Ron said with a slight chuckle. He attempted a smile, but his lips didn't quite cooperate. He hung his head for a moment and sucked in a deep breath of air before continuing. "Any idea what the news crews are doing here?

"I have no idea. I was gonna ask you guys the same question. Have you been contacted by any reporters?"

"No. We haven't been answering the home phone. We know it won't be long before they get their hands on our cell numbers, but for now we're maintaining a little privacy."

"Good. I'm sorry they're here at all. I can make sure they do not step foot onto church property, but I can't keep them from standing in the street and capturing video of everyone leaving the service. If you can delay the service a few more minutes, I'll make a couple calls to get more police out front."

"Sure Michael," Ron says as he retakes his seat next to Patty.

I turn to face the door once more and collect myself before getting to work.

Within minutes I have the perimeter of the property secure and I'm back inside the church sitting next to Ron and Patty. I try to stay in the moment to honor Michelle's memory, but my mind disobeys me and transports me back to my father's funeral. It was by far one of the hardest days of my life as I sat between my mother and Kate sobbing silently. I drop my head as the tears once again begin to roll for the loss of my father. Bruce Ayers was now a household name after he'd single handedly brought down the city's most corrupt businessmen from the grave. He was a local celebrity to the city of Charlotte, to me he was just Dad. A man that spent the last few years of his life turning me into the man I am today.

I feel a hand on my knee and turn to see my wife. I don't know when she arrived, but the sight of her took me even deeper into the memory of my father. It was the same touch of my knee that comforted me as the minister droned on about what a great man my father was. Now here I sit once again sobbing, only there's a teenage girl in the photos that adorn the front of the church. It's heart breaking and I decide in that moment to let all the pain flow out of me. Once I step outside of the walls of this church, I must be ready for war. Grieving for my father and Michelle needs to end here or Ron is going to spend the rest of his life in prison. After all he has been to me over the years, I'll die before I let that happen.

Chapter 7
Ryan

I stand next to Evan's bed watching him sleep. He's covered in bruises with tubes coming from everywhere. His head is wrapped in bandages and the machines are pumping an array of meds into him. Two hours after my last visit with him, he was attacked in his cell. No one at county lockup can tell me exactly what happened, but the working theory is that Evan was attacked by a group of inmates after they learned of the death of his daughter. As silly as it sounds, there is a code amongst criminals. Killing a child is one of the offenses that puts inmates in danger. Jail officials know this fact and should have done more to keep Evan safe. I'll be dealing with them after Evan recovers. The only bright side, if one could call it such, is that the attack led to the discovery of Evan's brain tumor. The meningioma brain tumor was a little larger than a golf ball and developed from the membrane that surrounds the brain and spinal cord. Although benign, the tumor blocked the brain's major drainage channel. After the beating he took, it's a sheer miracle Evan survived, or at the very least wasn't paralyzed or left with any permanent damage. The doctors expect Evan to make a full recovery.

I want to contact Lisa again to show her proof that Evan wasn't drinking when their daughter died. The neurosurgeon confirmed Evan has probably been in intolerable pain for weeks, possibly even months. The level of pain he must have been experiencing would leave a man barely able to string two words together, caring for a screaming infant would be nearly impossible. Without Evan's memories of that morning, no one can say for sure what happened. I have a theory though. I believe Evan got confused and placed the baby in the sink, instead of in her crib. That explains the bowl in the baby's crib. It was an accident, a terrible gut wrenching one, but that's all it was, an accident. Evan doesn't belong behind bars. Even as I recite the words over and over in my head, I know Lisa isn't the main person I need to convince. No, the thorn in my side, and hindrance to Evan's freedom was the prosecutor Bart Winslow.

Bart Winslow has a reputation for prosecuting even when there are clear signs of self-defense, or other mitigating circumstances. It was rumored that he was going to leave Charlotte and move down to Atlanta after the debacle he made of the Shamika Carrington case. It was the case that brought Charlotte, North Carolina to its knees. A young girl stabbed her father to death claiming he abused her for years and threatened to give her a backroom abortion. Bart prosecuted the case despite clear signs of abuse. In the end, it turned out that a person in a very high position of power and authority was involved in the exploitation of the girl. When the assailant's sins were uncovered, he snapped. Five people were killed that day and two were wounded. It was the bloodiest courtroom scene our state has ever experienced. As if the exploitation of the child were not enough, all sorts of corruption was uncovered.   Someone, whose name has yet to be publicly revealed, tried to prove Bart and his father conspired to wrongfully convict young Ms. Carrington, but the State Bar disagreed and allowed Bart to continue practicing law. One would think the embarrassment of such an accusation would encourage Bart to be more careful in deciding which cases to prosecute, but it seems Bart is a glutton for punishment. He prosecutes more than any other assistant district attorney in the state. I knew having him assigned to Evan's case meant trouble. Initially I thought about asking Michael to help me with this case because rumor has it, Bart's boss will not allow him to face off with Michael again. It would be great for Evan if I could get Michael involved, but I know asking for his help would be pointless. Michael now runs his own firm and is back to defending high dollar clients. Besides, Thomas would have a coronary and probably fire me. He hates Michael for stealing away one of the office's best lawyers. So here I stand, still hoping to spare my client prison time, but our chances went way down as soon as Bart was assigned to the case.

I notice movement out of the corner of my eye and turn to see Lisa Reynolds standing in the doorway. I watch her in silence as she ignores me and walks to the opposite side of the bed. I watch as she grabs Evan's hand and begins to speak to him as though I am not standing there.

"The doctors say your tumor had to have been growing for a while. I want to believe this whole thing is a nightmare, that my baby isn't gone, that you aren't to blame, but I can't. Tumor or not, you placed our daughter in a sink of water and she drowned to death. I've cried myself to sleep every night. I prayed and tried to find a way to forgive you. I want to, but I just can't. Every time I walk in the house, the house that we raised our family in, I'm bombarded by throat constricting grief. In time, I may be able to forgive you, but for now I can't. I just can't!"

As quickly as she came, Lisa Reynolds dropped her husband's hand and left the room. I stared down the hall until I could no longer see her. I turned to look at my client once more and saw tears streaming from both eyes. Not only was he awake, he heard every word.

***

I arrive home hoping to be able to hug my daughter before she goes to bed, but I am too late. Normally when I arrive late, I just glance at Kaitlin, but today I can't pass up a chance to hold her. I walk over and scoop her up into my arms. She nestles herself in to me and I inhale the scent of her shampoo as I take a seat in the rocker. Sitting here like this, holding her in a way she hasn't allowed since she could walk brings tears to my eyes. I think back to all the nights I rocked her as an infant. I think of all the times I watched my wife nurse our hungry daughter and hum to her as she sat in this same seat gently rocking. I'm not a fearful man, but I can't shake the fear that has gripped me since learning of the Reynolds' family tragedy. I can't imagine coming home one day and not finding her here. I close my eyes and try to stop Lisa Reynold's words from replaying over and over in my mind. No matter how hard I try, I can't dismiss the pain I heard in her words. Not only do I hear her pain, I feel it. I pull Kaitlin a little closer and she begins to writhe in protest. I know my limits. If Kaitlin wakes she won't allow me even a second of cuddle time so I release my hold and allow her to become comfortable without waking. I stare down at my strong-willed toddler and silently pray I never know the pain of losing her. I thank God for the opportunity to be her father and promise to always do my best to protect her. Then another thought intrudes. What makes me think Evan didn't do the same thing? Why has it been so easy for me to believe the worst about him since the very beginning? Because I'm cynical. The answer comes almost immediately. After defending so many guilty defendants over the years, it is very difficult to believe someone who lands in my stack of cases is actually innocent. Another very real truth about my profession is that I am not in the minority in this. This does nothing for the intense negative emotions I feel towards my job.

I stand and return Kaitlin to her bed. I don't want to hold my daughter and somehow feed my negative energy into her as she sleeps. I head towards the door and stop to take one final glance in her direction. I don't know if this is how Evan felt or not, but I know nothing on this planet could ever cause me to hurt my baby girl. The brain tumor could have been detected much sooner had Evan just gone to the doctor. Had he sought help, his baby girl would still be alive. I know I'm rationalizing at this point, but I can't stop myself. I'd eat a bullet before I let myself get so far gone that

Kaitlin would suffer. I can't understand any parent that wouldn't do the same.

I walk into our bedroom in time to catch Janice crawling into bed. She has that look in her eye that lets me know she wants to make love, but desire is nowhere near me tonight.

"I was wondering if you were ever going to remember your wife," Janice purrs.

"I just wanted to spend a little extra time with Kaitlin. I was bummed I didn't make it before she went to bed."

Janice senses the sadness in my voice. "What's wrong?"

"This case. Evan definitely had a brain tumor, but a baby is still dead. How can I help him stay out of prison when I know his daughter died at his hands?"

"Doesn't Thomas always say guilt or innocence has nothing to do with making sure the client get the best defense?"

"That's easy for him to say. He isn't the one putting baby killers back on the street. He hasn't actually defended a client in at least a decade."

"But if there was a brain tumor, Evan was sick. Should he be punished for something that was beyond his control?"

"Sick or not, his daughter is dead and his wife is heartbroken. Doesn't she deserve justice? And would you be so quick to defend me if it were Kaitlin?"

Janice moves closer to me and places both palms on my chest. She normally soothes me this way. I feel myself stiffen even more under her touch.

"You're an amazing father. If something happened to Kaitlin on your watch, I'd know without a shadow of doubt that you were completely blameless and I'd defend you until my dying breath."

I step away from her and turn to head towards our bathroom. "If something happened to Kaitlin on my watch, you'd have to bury both of us because I'd kill myself before nightfall," I say over my shoulder before I disappear behind the security of the bathroom door to continue wallowing in my despair.

Chapter 8
Michael

"I know you're under pressure to press charges, but this was an accident," I say to Landon McMurray, Charlotte's newly elected district attorney. After all the corruption my father revealed posthumously, the former DA resigned and Landon won a special election by a landslide. I know he's under pressure to run a tight ship, but I have to do everything I can to keep Ron out of prison.

"His daughter's death may have been an accident, but he beat Khalil Jeffries to death with his bare hands. I can't ignore the facts. Charlotte is a powder keg of racial tension. We're still recovering from the riots after the Keith Lamont Scott shooting. The city can't handle any more violence."

"So my client is supposed to be punished because CMPD killed an unarmed black man? That case has nothing to do with Ron."

"You're right. It doesn't, but Ron is a wealthy white man who beat a young black teenager to death."

"He thought Khalil was raping his daughter!"

"He was Michelle's boyfriend."

"How was Ron supposed to know that? Michelle was rebelling before her death. Ron and Patty hadn't even seen or heard from her for days. They didn't even know she was in the house. Imagine how you'd react if you went to sleep thinking you're home alone with your wife, but in the wee hours of the morning you're awakened by a female screaming."

"Michael, I understand you have to fight for your client. It's your job, but I also have a job. The media will spin this and we'll have a race war on our hands if I don't press charges."

"The media may also be interested to know you're willing to railroad an innocent man just to make yourself look good to the race baiters," I say with more venom than I intend to show.

"Taking a page from your old man's book huh?" Landon challenges. "Bruce Ayers may still be the subject of gossip for what he did, but make no mistake, you're not your father. If you go to the media with this, you'll be sorry. Now, you can convince your client to surrender himself for processing, or I can have CMPD go to his office. And Michael....if you make me do that, I will make sure the media is there."

I stand realizing I've been beaten. Landon isn't going to back down, but that's okay. There's more than one way to get him to see things my way. Ron has been there for me for as long as I can remember. I'm not letting him go to prison.

"Give us 48 hours to get things in order with his company & he'll surrender," I say knowing the request will be denied.

"Either he surrenders by close of business tomorrow, or I'll have CMPD arrest him in front of every news crew in the city."

"So, that's how you're going to play this? You're going to be an intentional hard ass? Haven't you ever needed someone to cut you a little slack?"

"Sure I have, but I never beat a child to death with my bare hands. 5 pm Michael, 5:01 and Ron will be paraded in front of the cameras. Oh...and you should know, Bart won't be assigned to this. I'm handling the trial personally."

***

I sit in front of Ron choking back tears as I explain my meeting with McMurray. Ron is much calmer than I expect, but I can still see the pain in his eyes. His red rimmed eyes are dry, not the typical no-tears type of dry...more like no-tears-left-to-cry type of dry. He just buried his only child, his miracle baby...he shouldn't be dealing with this right now. Yet, here we are attempting to make sure his business will survive the impending legal crisis he is about to endure.

"McMurray has promised not to include the media if we surrender by close of business tomorrow. Do you think you can get everything handled in time?"

"I don't trust McMurray. He's just another politician trying to make a name for himself. I'm prepared to surrender today."

I don't hide the surprise on my face or in my voice. "How are you prepared to surrender when I just gave you the information?"

"Michael, please don't take this the wrong way. I have every faith in your abilities as an attorney, but I never leave my fate totally in anyone else's hands. I have a source that's keeping me in the loop."

I sit back in my chair trying to keep my thoughts at bay. I can't listen to them right now, no matter how loud they scream at me. I take a calming breath before I speak again.

"Ron, please don't tell me you've done anything illegal like bribe someone to tell you what's going on."

Ron laughs a hearty laugh, a laugh that sounds like the Ron of yesteryear. It's the first I've heard of its kind since before that awful phone call. "No Michael. I didn't bribe anyone. I have a lot of friends all over this city. With that in mind, I think I have a way out of this.

Trust me when I say you're not going to like it and you don't want to know the details."

I lean forward. "What are you talking about Ron?"

"I'm going to plead guilty."

I jump to my feet. "Like hell you are! You are not going to prison Ron. I know you're feeling guilty about Michelle, but you don't belong behind bars. You thought your daughter was being raped and you did what any decent father would do. I can't believe we're even having this conversation! How the hell could you even consider this?"

Ron holds up his hand signaling for me to stop speaking. "I'm not going to prison. I'm going to plead guilty to involuntary manslaughter and I want you to rush for me to be sentenced as quickly as possible."

I take my seat again, now intrigued by what Ron is saying to me. "Ron, I know you think you have a plan, but you aren't an attorney. First, you're assuming you'll be charged with involuntary manslaughter. I just spoke with Landon McMurray, I can assure you he intends to charge you with second degree murder for Khalil Jeffries. We may be able to negotiate Michelle's death down to involuntary manslaughter, but the D.A. was very clear where Khalil is concerned. He's afraid there will be more rioting if you aren't brought to justice."

"Michael, you let me worry about McMurray. You just start working on your statements for my sentencing hearing. I'd like an opportunity to speak as well."

I shake my head in disagreement. "Ron, listen to me. What you're suggesting is not only stupid, but it could backfire. You can't determine what you'll plead guilty to until the D.A. presses charges. You don't get to decide that."

"Michael, trust me. I know what I'm doing."

"How can I trust you when I don't know what you're doing? You hired me to be your attorney. You need to trust me and listen to my advice. Even if by some miracle you are charged with involuntary manslaughter on both counts, you could still face lengthy consecutive sentences. Some of the judges around here are known for giving the maximum sentences allowed."

"I'm done discussing it Michael. I haven't gotten this far in business by not remaining one step ahead of my enemies. Remember what I used to tell you when you were a kid?"

I stare at Ron incredulously. He told me many things as a kid, none of which seems to apply here. "You told me a lot of things," I say with a pout in my voice that I haven't heard since I was ten.

"Always be the smartest man in the room, Michael. Always be the smartest man in the room. I know what I'm doing. I made a horrible mistake that night, but I'm going to outsmart McMurray and put all of this behind me. I'll meet you downstairs at 3pm sharp. I want to get there early enough to be released before dinner."

Again, I stare at Ron wondering where the tender man that let the kid next door spend countless hours at his house has gone. The man before me is cold and calculating. If not for the red rimmed eyes, I would not believe I was talking to a grieving father. "Ron, there is no guarantee you'll be out before dinner. You'll have to meet with the magistrate for bail to be decided. That takes hours, especially in the evenings."

"I'll be home before dinner. Be here at 3 so we can get this over with."

Chapter 9
Ryan

I sit waiting for Bartholomew "Bart" Winslow to end his phone call while struggling to keep my anger in check. Bart has basically ignored my presence for the last five minutes. He's continued a phone call that I'm fairly certain could have ended the minute I arrived. After all, it isn't as though I showed up unannounced. We planned this meeting a week ago, the same day Evan was released from the hospital. Bart even called me. He requested the meeting, yet he sits here now intentionally ignoring me. I may be a rookie, but I have pride. I stand and start to leave when I hear Bart call out to me.

"Ryan, come back."

I turn around and look at an amused Bart. Was this his idea of a joke? Does he find pleasure in wasting my time? I'm no longer able to hold my anger in. "Do you think it's funny to waste my time? I have better things to do than sit here watching you hold unnecessary phone conversations. If you want an audience that bad, make one of the interns around here watch you, but do not waste my time."

Bart stands and smiles. "Relax. It was just a little hazing. Everyone has gone through it."

His response does nothing to quell my anger. In fact, it makes me angrier. "Look, this isn't a high school locker room. This is real life. People's futures are in our hands. I don't play games. If that's what you want, go find someone else to play with."

Bart's expression hardens. "I see Thomas has gotten his hooks buried deep into you. He turns everyone that works for him into legal puppets with no sense of humor."

I take my seat. "This isn't about Thomas. You called me here to talk about my client Evan Reynolds. Let's talk about him."

Bart sits as well. "If that's how you want it, let's talk about the baby killer. I'm charging him with second degree murder."

"What! How the hell can you justify that? This was an accident."

"You call it an accident. I call it a grave disregard for human life."

"Evan had a brain tumor that was causing him so much pain he blacked out. He has no memory of that morning, but he loved his daughter. He would have never intentionally placed her in harm's way."

"Brain tumor or not, a baby died on your client's watch. He conveniently doesn't remember what happened, but his wife remembers him being so drunk that he could barely get out of the bed."

"And you're not charging her for leaving her baby at home with a drunk man? Isn't that child endangerment or neglect?"

"In light of the circumstances, and her agreement to testify against her husband, Lisa Reynolds will not face any charges. She's a grieving mother that wants to see justice for her daughter so she can move on with her life. Besides, we can reasonably assume Lisa did not realize Evan would hurt their daughter. He raised their other three children without incident. Given his previous role as a loving father, there was no endangerment or neglect on Lisa's part. She believed her husband was capable of caring for their daughter. Unfortunately, she was wrong and is paying for her mistake in the worse way possible."

"Paying for her mistake, huh? What you're really saying is, Lisa will make a better witness because people will side with the mother over the father. In case you forgot, Evan's grieving too. He had nothing to gain from killing his daughter. He's a loving father. He's not a murderer. And besides, I saw the lab results. Evan's blood alcohol level was zero. He wasn't drinking."

"That test means nothing. According to the medical examiner, baby Ciara had been dead for several hours before Lisa Reynolds found her in the sink. After all that time, of course Evan's blood alcohol level was zero."

"So rather than taking the word of a grieving father, you charge him with murder? Come on Bart, do the right thing. You know this is manslaughter at best."

"I don't know that. I believe Lisa Reynolds, the hard-working nurse that spends hours saving lives only to come home and find her own daughter drowned to death in her kitchen sink while her husband lay in a drunken stupor."

"So you already have the narrative planned, huh? You basically chose the parent who'd be most sympathetic. Well, don't underestimate the love of a father. You're forgetting Evan and Lisa have three older children that love both of their parents. They'll testify that there's no way their father could have intentionally drowned their baby sister." I don't know if anything I just said about the older children is true, but it doesn't matter. I'm only laying the bait to see if Bart will bite and tell me whether or not he's already spoken with the older three children. His smile tells me he's so arrogant that he can't pass up the chance to gloat.

"I've already spoken to the older children. They will testify that their father has been drinking more and more over the last two years. They barely recognize him now."

I stand realizing I've gained all I need from Bart. I know where I need to turn for help. It's a long shot, but I have to try. I don't necessarily know how I feel about Evan. I still can't comprehend letting anything happen to my daughter, but it's my job to make sure he doesn't get railroaded by an overzealous ADA who only cares about putting people behind bars. Bart needs to be stopped and I know exactly how to do it.

***

Sitting in Michael's office waiting for him gave me an opportunity to admire my surroundings. Michael's corner office was at least three times larger than mine. Pictures of him and Kate adorned his credenza along with pictures of an older woman I assume to be his mother. There's also a picture of Bruce Ayers, Michael's father and the man that built Michael's firm and made sure Michael would be the sole partner after his death. The final picture is of two African American females along with a young boy. I instantly know who they are and I smile. Michael may be defending high dollar clients again, but that hasn't stopped him from maintaining contact with Shamika and her family. Maybe thinking Michael will help me with Evan's case isn't so farfetched after all.

Michael walks into his office and as I stand to shake his hand, the look on his face tells me I have no chance whatsoever. I'm already here so I give it my best shot knowing he's going to say no.

"Hi Michael. You probably don't remember me, but we worked together during your time at the public defender's office."

"I remember you," he says without even looking at me. "You interrupted Thomas during my first morning meeting and asked him if he was going to introduce me."

I'm shocked he remembered such a minute detail. "Yes," I say with a slight chuckle. "That was me. I'm surprised you remember that."

"I remember everything about that day. It was one of the worst days of my life. So... why are you here? If you're looking for a job, I'm not hiring any new associates right now. Although, it would be nice to stick it to Thomas by hiring more talent from under him, we're fully staffed right now."

"Actually, I'm not looking for a job. I might need one if Thomas finds out I came to you for help, but right now I just need help, not a job."

"What exactly do you need my help with?"

"Well...I'm sure you've seen the news. The man charged with drowning his infant daughter, Evan Reynolds, Thomas assigned me to his case. Bart is the prosecutor and he's charging the guy with 2nd degree murder when it was clearly an accident. It's manslaughter at best."

"And you think I can help because I have history with Bart?"

"You have a history of beating Bart. Plus, I know you're a great attorney and you care about seeing the judicial process work as intended. I think you hate seeing innocent clients being unfairly charged and prosecuted as much as I do."

"How do you know this Evan guy didn't intentionally drown his daughter?"

"It's a gut feeling. He's a father. I'm a father. I know the bond between a father and his daughter. There's no way a decent man would drown his own daughter."

"Who says this guy is a decent man? Look Ryan, I'd love to help you, but I've seen the news. I can't say that I'm convinced this is a miscarriage of justice, and even if it were, I have my own case that is going to take up most of my time. I can't take on anything else right now."

"Michael, I'd do all of the work. I just need you to help look over a couple of the motions and sit second chair. Just seeing your name listed as opposing counsel will help. I heard McMurray won't let Bart face off against you anymore. If I get Bart removed from this case, I'm sure I can keep my client out of prison."

Michael throws his head back and laughs loudly. "Stop believing the gossip. Bart and I haven't faced off since the Carrington case, but McMurray won't hesitate to pit Bart against me again. My name won't help your case, it'll hurt it. Bart will become far more viscous with me involved. You're better off handling this one solo. Besides, I'm sure your client can't afford our fees."

I hang my head visibly disappointed. "I thought you might consider taking the case pro bono."

Michael laughs again. "I'm a nice guy, but I don't do pro bono. That time working at the public defender's office was enough free legal work for me for a lifetime. Now, I don't mean to be rude, but I have a 3 o'clock appointment that I can't be late for."

Michael stands and extends his hand. I shake it and watch as he leaves me standing in his office. I turn to leave the building, but another thought occurs to me. At this point, I don't have anything to lose, so instead of leaving I turn and head in the direction of the second best lawyer in the firm.

Chapter 10
Michael

Following my short meeting with Ryan Du Bois, I head over to Ron's office. Ron's company specializes in business acquisition and occupies the most expansive suite of offices downtown Charlotte has to offer. Finding a parking space in front of the building is impossible after the security changes the city made post 9-11, but Ron's company offers valet parking. I pull up in front of the valet stand expecting to exit my car, when I see Ron walking out the front door at 3pm on the dot. His expression is much lighter than I expect for a man about to turn himself in to authorities. When he climbs into my car I can't stop myself from asking the obvious question.

"Ron, why are you so calm about this?"

"I know the outcome Michael."

It's at that moment that it all sets in. I bring the car to a complete stop at a red light and turn to face Ron. "I don't know what you did or think you did, but I can't be involved in anything illegal. I have a kid on the way and a law firm full of employees depending on me for their paychecks. If what you're doing might bring repercussions to my front door, I need to excuse myself as your attorney."

Ron stares at me for so long that I wonder if he'll respond at all. The car behind me honks their horn. I turn to see the light is green and begin driving again. The silence in the car is pregnant with anticipation and speculation. We continue this way until Ron finally responds.

"Michael I can't see how this will affect you in any way. I'm not committing any crimes, but I have done business in this city for many years. I've been careful to make the right alliances, and give to the right charities. I've been generous in my local business dealings and I've brought a substantial amount of business to the city. I've helped to negotiate the attraction of every professional sports team the city has the pleasure of enjoying. I sit on several influential boards across several industries. In short, my ties and dedication to this community are strong. Those ties are going to ensure my freedom. If you want to distance yourself from me, I'll understand. You have to do what is best for you and the future of your family and business. There won't be any hard feelings if you walk away."

Ron's words touch me and my mind travels once again to all the nights he and Patty made time for me when my own parents were busy with galas and fundraisers benefiting inner city children. Their own child needed attention and thanks to the man sitting next to me, I received it.

"I'll be right here Ron."

***

I've never been known for my ability to hide my emotions. As I watch Ron's plan unfold, I remain true to my character. My face displays every emotion I feel as Ron waltzes into the Mecklenburg County jail, surrenders himself, waits to see a magistrate, and is released in less than an hour. There was no time in a holding cell, nor heckling or stalling from the sheriff's deputies. Everyone did their job efficiently and gave Ron more respect than I've ever seen given to any offender. As much as I hate to admit it, the egotistical side of me loved watching a powerful man control a system whose sole purpose is to control.

During our ride to Ron's home, he chats lightly about his daughter and how much he is going to miss having her around. I notice the sadness in his voice has been replaced by the fondness I'd seen in the years before Michelle's death. His daughter is barely cold in her grave and Ron is already moving to the acceptance phase of the grief process. I admonish myself for thinking such thoughts, but given his disposition and the way he's handling the criminal charges, which by the way were two counts of involuntary manslaughter just as Ron said they'd be, I'm left scratching my head. I'm not comfortable with the situation, but my life feels like one big debt that I owe to Ron and Patty. I feel guilty for questioning how Ron grieves and for how long. My son hasn't even been born yet, and I'd probably strangle anyone that questioned my love for him.

After dropping Ron off at home and promising to get to work on pushing his sentencing hearing as quickly as possible, I head home. It's been an incredibly exhausting day and I want nothing more than to get home to my wife. We haven't been seeing much of each other these days, mostly because of our work schedules, but also because she's still mad at me. It seems I can do nothing to please her these days. I'm praying the little blue box I had Tanya leave on her desk has gotten me out of the dog house.

I enter our home and notice it's completely dark which means Kate hasn't made it home yet. I glance at my watch. It's only ten after five which is early for either of us to get home. I head to the fridge and decide to cook the pork chops Kate has been defrosting in the fridge. New jewelry and coming home to a nice home cooked meal will definitely put Kate in the mood to forgive me. I wash the meat while the oven pre-heats and find a pan to bake it in. I'm a southern boy at heart and would love nothing more than to fry these chops and smother them in gravy, but Kate is much more health conscious than I am, so oven baked pork chops it is. Once the meat is in the oven, I look for veggies to go with them.

I settle on a salad since it's fast and again, I know Kate will like it.

With a few extra minutes on my hands, I decide to shower while the meat bakes. Just as I lather my hair with shampoo, I hear the chime of the alarm system signaling the arrival of my wife. I quickly rinse and exit the shower. I grab a towel and dry off. I don't bother wrapping the towel around me. I step into our bedroom naked as the day I was born ready to rekindle the romance with my wife, but the sight of her stops me dead in my tracks.

Kate is crying. Not silent tears running down her face because she saw something sad on television type crying. No, Kate is sobbing uncontrollably as she throws clothing into a suitcase on the bed. My mind races into a thousand different directions as I watch my life slipping away from me. Make no mistake, Kate is the center of my world. She is the main reason I get up in the mornings. Before she came back into my life, I had no clue what my purpose for living was, now I have no clue how I could ever live without her. She can't leave me.

"Kate, what the hell? What's wrong? Why are you packing?"

"I can't do this anymore Michael. I need a minute to catch my breath."

"What the hell are you talking about?"

"I can't watch you revert back to the same arrogant asshole you used to be. I didn't agree to marry a heartless bastard."

"Hold up! What are you talking about?" I grab Kate by the arm and swing her around so that she's facing me.

Kate slaps me hard, and I immediately release her. "Don't you ever grab me like that again."

My hand goes instantly to my stinging cheek. "So it's okay for you to slap the shit out of me, but it's not okay for me to touch your arm? That's bullshit and you know it."

"You didn't just touch my arm. You grabbed me and jerked me around. I'm not some helpless low self-esteem bimbo you can control."

"So now we're back to that? You think I'm that guy? So the past year I've spent treating you like the fucking queen of England went out the window the second I didn't measure up to some invisible standard you set for me. I don't even know what I did!"

"And that's the problem Mike. You never know what you've done. You just go around hurting people and leaving a trail of sorrow without giving a second thought to the feelings of the people you interact with."

Now not only am I confused, I'm pissed at her accusation. "Look I know I'm not as perfect as Saint Kate, but I am a decent man. I do my best to live up to this morality bullshit you keep throwing at me, but it's never good enough for you. No matter what I do you keep accusing me of being someone that I'm clearly not."

"I'm not accusing you of anything. I'm facing reality. I'm married to a man that will happily defend someone who beats a defenseless teenager to death with his bare hands, but won't spare ten minutes for the poor guy whose daughter accidentally drowned."

"Is that what this is about? You're pissed because I wouldn't work on Ryan's case? You know how swamped I am with Ron's defense right now. Like it or not, Ron and Patty are like second parents to me. I'm not going to let him go to prison. And which cases I take have nothing to do with who I am as a man and a husband."

"That's where we disagree," Kate says as she stuffs the last item into her suitcase and zips it shut. "The cases you accept tell me exactly who you are. I'm moving out until you can see that."

I stand silently fuming while my reason for living walks out of our home, with our future growing in her belly.

Chapter 11
Ryan

I walk into the house just as Janice is putting the last of what I assume was dinner into Tupperware containers. I expect to hear Kaitlin's feet as they pad across the hardwoods to greet me, but the house is silent. Janice doesn't even look up to acknowledge me. I know I'm late, but late arrivals are fairly common in our household. They typically don't bother Janice. I drop my keys onto the table near the door and sit my briefcase on the floor next to it. Something is off.

"Hey," I say to my wife in what I hope is a light and jovial tone.

"We need to talk."

Instantly I feel my anger rise. Janice knows how much I loathe those words she uses when she wants to tell me something that is likely to wreck my world. We've talked about this more times than I'd like to recall. I've asked her to just start talking. She insists it's hard for her to start difficult conversations and those four ridiculous words strewn together are her opener. I'm not in the mood for a big argument today. After meeting with Kate, I left work on a high note, I don't want to be pulled back to the pit of despair that held me hostage last night.

"You know how I feel about those words."

Janice looks at me apologetically and I breathe a sigh of relief knowing she didn't intend to start a fight. I feel my anger extinguishing.

"I'm sorry. You know I'm trying but that's how I've started serious conversations my whole life."

I walk over to my wife and place my arms around her. I hug her close to me and hold her for much longer than customary. My embrace always seems to relax her and I can tell we both need to relax before we discuss whatever is on her mind. Janice lays her head on my chest and neither of us speaks until I feel her begin to shutter. I pull back and look into my wife's tear filled eyes.

"Baby what's wrong?"

That sends my wife into a full sob fest. She buries her head into my chest again and cries uncontrollably. She's so upset she begins to frighten me.

"Is it Kaitlin? Where is she? Is she okay?"

"Kaitlin is fine. She's with my mom. I didn't want her here for this."

I pull away again. "Janice what are you talking about?"

"I didn't mean for any of this to happen. I love you and I don't want to lose you. It all just happened so subtly and things got out of control."

I step away from Janice completely. I don't like what I just heard and I can't touch her if she's about to tell me what I think she's trying to tell me. She breaks down again when I move away. I'm not sure if I want her to continue shattering my world, so I don't urge her to continue. I stand there watching her sob into her hands until she begins to speak again.

"I've been seeing Clifton."

Everything inside of me breaks as soon as the words leave her mouth. Janice is what I consider to be the perfect wife. She's not actually perfect, but I always thought she was perfect for me. Now she's telling me she's been having an affair with her boss. She reaches out to me, but I jerk away before she can connect. I don't want her to touch me. I don't want to even look at her. I turn and head upstairs without replying. I'm afraid of what I might say or do if I open my mouth. I hear Janice behind me, but I can't make out anything she's saying. My blood is pulsing louder and louder in my ears with each step, effectively drowning her out. By the time I reach our bedroom I'm starting to see red. I need to grab some items from the closet and get out of the house before I do something I'll regret. Janice is still there but I can barely even hear her voice now. I grab a suitcase and start absent mindedly throwing things into it. I'm not even sure if I've grabbed things that match, and I don't care. I just have to get out of the house before I explode.

I zip the suitcase and head downstairs. I stop at the door to the garage when I see Janice standing in front of it. I don't know when she left the bedroom, but I know I'm not doing this with her. Just looking at her makes me want to do something I'll regret. I walk

towards her and see relief wash over her face. She's
mistaken what's happening. I don't open my mouth to
correct her. I grab my keys and briefcase, and turn to
walk out of the front door. I hear Janice behind me.
She says something about Kaitlin. My daughter's name
is the only thing that registers. I stop and turn to face
her. I take in her swollen red face and open my mouth
to speak for the first time since she uttered those awful,
marriage ending words, but quickly change my mind.
Without a word, I head out the front door. Janice is on
my heels all the way to the garage. She beats on my
window yelling through tears as I back out of the
garage. I turn the radio on and blast it to drown out the
lingering sounds of her babbling and leave our
driveway as fast as I can.

The drive to Janice's mom's house was shorter than
usual, but I couldn't waste time getting to Kaitlin. If
Janice thought she was going to tear our family apart
and keep custody of our daughter, she was sorely
mistaken. I walk up the front steps and ring the
doorbell fully prepared to fight for my daughter. To my
surprise, Janice's mother opens the door with a
sleeping Kaitlin in her arms. She smiles warmly at me.

"Hi Ryan. I was just about to move her from the sofa to the guestroom when you rang the bell. Good thing you did too, because this little girl is getting too old for Nana to carry."

Janice's mom chuckles. Her light and cheerful tone tells me she has no idea what's going on with Janice and me. I decide to play along.

"Yeah, looks like I got here just in time to prevent you from having a backache tomorrow. Do you have her bag? I wanna go ahead and get her home and into bed."

"Sure, it's right over here."

The phone rings and my heart leaps into my chest. I'm sure it's Janice. I know her so well. I'm sure she's calling to ask her mom if she'll watch Kaitlin overnight. There's no way she'll be able to pull herself together enough to care for our daughter tonight. I quickly grab Kaitlin's bag and head for the door. I don't want to be here when Janice talks to her mom.

"Thanks for watching Kaitlin Mom. I'll see you later."

I rush out the front door and down the steps to my car. The engine is still running as I strap my daughter into her car seat. By the time I get to the driver's side door, my mother-in-law is on her porch yelling at me, telling me Janice said for me not to take Kaitlin. I wave and smile as though I didn't understand what she said. I put my car in reverse and back out of the driveway without bothering to glance back at the porch.

Kaitlin and I arrive at the Marriott City Center and get settled into our room. I get Kaitlin tucked into bed without her ever waking. I've never been more grateful to have a child that can sleep through anything. As I shower, the weight of the day settles on me and I let the tears fall down the drain, praying they'll take the hollow feeling in the pit of my stomach with them. I've dedicated most of my adult life to Janice, the thought of her being in the arms of her sleazy boss makes me heave. I turn the water off and exit the shower. I stand in front of the toilet waiting for the heaving to stop. I realize nothing is actually coming up because I haven't eaten since lunch. I throw on my pajama bottoms and head back into the room prepared to order room service. I locate the menu and call down to order a burger and fries. I consider cracking open a few bottles from the mini bar, but I decide not to drink just in case Kaitlin wakes up confused by her strange surroundings.

Twenty minutes later there is a knock on the door. I open it without bothering to look through the peep hole. I instantly regret that decision. Standing next to the room service waiter stands Janice. She looks like she hasn't stopped crying, but there is a strong undertone of anger in her expression. I pull the room service table into the room myself and hand the waiter his tip. He looks surprised by me not allowing him into the room, but doesn't ask any questions. He simply takes his money and walks away. I try to close the door, but Janice sticks her foot out preventing me from shutting her out.

"Janice, I'm exhausted and starving. I don't have the energy to do this with you right now."

"Then let me in so we can talk about this like adults. You can't just run off with my daughter without saying anything to me."

"What's there to say? You slept with Clifton, end of story."

"No it's not the end of the story. And who said I slept with him?

"You did!"

"I never said that! In fact, I said the opposite. I chased you around the house and embarrassed myself in front of the nosey neighbors trying to tell you we didn't sleep together."

"Then what the hell did you say? Because I heard you say you've been fucking him!" I yell much louder than I intend to. I regret letting her force me to talk as soon as I hear Kaitlin begin to whine. I walk away from the door and go comfort our daughter. I know Janice is following me and I don't care. I don't have the energy to fight her.

I scoop Kaitlin into my arms relieved to see she's not completely awake. She wiggles until she gets comfortable against me. Neither one of us speaks until Kaitlin is sound asleep again. As soon as I lay my daughter back down and tuck her in, I move to the table and begin eating my now cold burger and fries.

"Are you going to keep ignoring me and making things up in your head or are you going to hear me out?"

"Janice, I'm tired. I heard all I needed to hear earlier. I left the house before I did something stupid so I could process this. You followed me all around the house, now you've followed me here. You're insisting on having this your way which points to how selfish you are. How the hell did you find me anyway?"

"I used the *Find My iPhone* app. You took my daughter and wouldn't answer the phone. What was I supposed to do?"

"She's not *YOUR* daughter, she's our daughter. I wanted to have her close to me because you and I both know the judge will probably award you physical custody. I wanted her close to me tonight. You weren't going to pick her up in your condition. What harm is it for me to have her with me?"

"You could have talked to me. What was I supposed to think?"

"What you think is no longer my concern. You lost that place when you broke my heart."

"Come on Ryan. I made a mistake. You could at least hear me out. You owe me that much."

"I owe you? Did you just say I owe you? I've given the last ten years of my life to you. I practically worship the ground you walk on and you have the nerve to say I owe you! Get out Janice."

"I'm not going anywhere without my daughter."

"Janice, so help me God, if you don't get out of this room, I'm going to drag you out."

Janice breaks down in tears again. "Please Ryan, just let me explain. I promise I'll go if you just let me explain."

"Dammit Janice! Don't you get it? You don't get to call the shots on this one. Give me some time to digest this and I'll decide if and when we talk. Until then, get the hell out and give me some space," my chest is rapidly moving up and down as I struggle to get a handle on my anger. My hands are shaking. I managed to keep my voice down, but I'm not sure I can keep this up much longer.

Janice finally gives in and starts to head towards the door. "Will you at least promise me you'll bring Kaitlin home tomorrow?"

I sigh. "Yes, Janice. I'll make sure she's home early enough to eat breakfast with you."

"Will you stay for breakfast as well?"

"Don't count on it."

Chapter 12
Michael

My sadness has now been replaced by anger and I have no plans whatsoever to beg my wife to come back to me. I love Kate, but I'm not going to spend the rest of my life under the scrutiny of her disapproving stare. I head into the office fully prepared to ignore her presence. There's a good chance I'll go the whole day without even seeing her. That would really be best for both of us. As upset as she was last night, she should take the day to rest. I know her well though, there's no chance she'll miss work today. Kate's first love will always be the clients. I knew this when we reconnected, but somehow I believed this would change after we were married. I was wrong.

"Good morning Michael," Tanya smiles with her greeting as she rushes up to me.

I've just walked in the door, the last thing I want to do is deal with Tanya and her aggressive flirting. "Good morning Tanya. I'm not in the mood to be manipulated this morning. Stop trying to flirt with me and just tell me what you want."

Tanya's smile does not fade. In fact, it grows wider, if that's even possible. "I'm not trying to flirt with you, but I do want to work on the Edahl case."

I stop and turn to face Tanya. "Why would you want to work on Ron's case?"

"I've been with you for almost a year and all I've been assigned are simple cut and dry cases. When you hired me, you said you believed I had what it took to go from legal secretary to lawyer. I'm looking to start law school in the very near future and experience working on a criminal trial defense team will be good practice for me."

"I agree it would be great practice, but there is no trial here. Ron is going to plead guilty so that he can be sentenced as soon as possible."

Tanya's smile finally fades. "Why would he do that? Doesn't he understand he'll spend the rest of his life behind bars?"

"I explained all of that to him. His mind is made up."

"You have to make him change it!"

My forehead creases involuntarily. "I'm shocked to see you so passionate about this case. You've never shown an interest in any of our clients before. What's different about this one?"

Tanya's expression is unreadable. "Nothing. I just spent time researching similar cases already. I had my hopes up."

"If you want trial experience so bad, go speak with Kate. She has a new case that you can probably help with. I'm sure they'll be filing plenty of motions you can help draft."

Tanya's expression does not lighten. "And you're sure Ron Edahl is just going to plead guilty?"

"Yes. What am I missing here Tanya? You're too interested in this case."

Tanya tries to recover by telling me once again that she's just sad she put time into preliminary research work for nothing. I don't believe her for a second. Everything in me is telling me to keep an eye on her.

***

Half way through the morning, my desk phone rings.

"This is Michael."

"Michael, this is Landon."

I'm shocked to hear the DA on the other end of the line. "Hey Landon. What can I do for you?"

"For starters, you can tell your client I think he's a lowlife son of a bitch and if it were up to me he'd never breathe free air again."

"Excuse me? What the hell are you talking about?"

"Don't pretend you don't know what your piece of shit client did."

"I honestly have no clue what's going on. He's my client, but he doesn't have to tell me everything."

"I don't believe that. This has your fingerprints all over it. You both think you've won. You think you've pulled off one of the greatest legal maneuvers of all time, but I promise you I will have the last laugh."

"Seriously Landon, I have no idea what you're talking about..."

"Give it a rest," Landon demands. "Just have your child killer present for his preliminary hearing tomorrow."

"We're waiving preliminary."

"Then file the damn paperwork so we can move forward."

Landon McMurray slams the phone down in my ear. I don't have much experience with Landon as he hasn't been the DA very long, but he has an impeccable reputation for his professionalism and strict adherence to the rules. The person that just hung up on me sounds nothing like the man I've heard so much about.

As morning turns to afternoon, the day passes like one huge blur. I can't remember much of what happened between my phone call with McMurray and this moment when my wife walks into my office and closes the door behind her.

"I didn't expect to see you today," I say without any of the love that is usually reserved for my wife.

Kate sits down in front of me. "I didn't expect to come see you. Nadine convinced me to sit down and explain my point of view to you."

I think of several snappy ways to respond, but I decide it would be better for me to remain silent. Kate continues.

"I was wrong for blowing up on you last night. I should have said something sooner. I've been letting this fester for a while and the pregnancy hormones just threw me into crazy overload."

"You've been letting what fester?"

"I love you Mike. I've loved you since college. I knew you and I didn't see eye to eye on some social issues, but this past year working together has shown me a side of you that bothers me."

"Kate, you knew who I was before you married me. I never hid my background from you. I've been completely transparent."

"I know. I think I hoped your bond with Shamika changed you."

"It did change me. Before Shamika and getting you back, I only cared about myself. I didn't do anything unless it benefited me personally. I'm not that person anymore."

"But you lack empathy Mike. You see injustice and just keep moving like it isn't happening in front of you. Don't get me wrong. You are wonderful with me, and Shamika, and even Nadine; but we are people you care about. You have a personal relationship with each of us. When it comes to strangers you are content sitting on the sidelines while someone suffers, even when you have the power to step in and right the wrong."

"What does that have to do with us? You just admitted I treat you well. I've given you more of me than anyone else will ever see. We're having a baby for crying out loud."

"My decision to agree to have a baby has nothing to do with my concerns. I always knew you'd be an amazing father. You're missing the point."

"What's the point?" My voice is now elevated because I'm frustrated with this conversation. Kate is speaking in riddles and I'm sick of it.

"The point is I don't know if I can stay married to a man that readily turns his back on injustice without giving the victims a second thought."

"Kate, I can't save the world. I'm concerned about the people I love. You're right, I don't think about injustices strangers face. It's not intentional, I just don't think about them. I'm not wired that way."

"That's a problem for me Mike. So much of who I am is tied to my passion for justice and proper counsel for the less fortunate. How can I be married to someone who doesn't share this core belief?"

"I can't change who I am. I wasn't raised to recognize the plight of the less fortunate like you were. I was a millionaire before I was born. My father was a lawyer, so I followed in his footsteps so that I could one day take over the family business. The law is just a profession for me, not a crusade for righteousness. Clients hire me to do a job. I do that job and move on to the next. That's who I am as an attorney. As a husband and father, I'll always love and protect you. I'll provide for you and assure you never experience an ounce of pain that I can prevent. I've pledged my life to ensure you and our future children live beautiful lives and know without question that I'll always be there for you. I can't change who I am for you Kate. I wish I could be as passionate about helping the less fortunate as you are, but I can't."

"What about Shamika?"

"What about her?"

"Doesn't she make you want to make sure no other little girls experience the hell she experienced?"

"While I was in the middle of her case, yes. But honestly, after life got back to normal I don't think about the others anymore. I love Shamika like I'll love my own daughter one day so I'll still do anything in my power to protect her, but I can't save the world Kate. I can't go looking for Shamikas that need saving. Her case was the single most emotionally draining case of my career. If I worked on cases like that all the time, I wouldn't have anything left to offer you or our children."

"I know you're right, which is why this is so difficult. I don't think I can be married to someone who doesn't have the ability to match my capacity to champion cases and causes for the less fortunate. You come from money. I was poor. I know what it feels like to feel helpless because someone is exploiting your circumstance."

"What are you talking about? Your parents aren't poor."

"My parents are comfortable now. They weren't always. And that's not the point. The point is, I need a mate who understands and participates in righteously defending the poor, not someone who sells his soul to the highest bidder."

I'm saddened by her last remark. I can tell she didn't say it to hurt me, but it still stung.

"I love you Kate, but I am who I am. I'm working to become a better man so that I can be someone our son will be proud of, but I don't know if I'll ever live up to your expectations."

Kate stands without looking up to meet my stare. "I understand. I feel guilty for even bringing it up. I have no right to try to change you. I think it's best if I stay at Nadine's a little longer. I need time and space to sort through my feelings."

"You don't have to do that. I can flop at the condo. You can stay at home so you and the baby will be comfortable."

"No. Nadine's place is fine. I can't bear the thought of sleeping in our bed alone."

"Neither can I."

Kate leaves the office and I can tell by the rise and fall of her shoulders that she's crying. There's nothing I can do to ease her pain. I could lie and tell her I'm going to magically morph into the man she wants me to be, but lying will only prolong the inevitable. In the long run we'd both end up in a much worse situation. In hind sight, I knew going into this marriage, I wasn't the man she really wanted or deserved. Like everything else in my life though, I selfishly accepted her as mine even when I knew I didn't deserve her.

Chapter 13
Ryan

It's been two weeks since Janice ripped our world apart. We're falling into a rhythm. I see Kaitlin every other evening. She hasn't been back to the hotel after that first night. Mostly because I don't want to confuse her, but also because I've needed the time alone. More often than not, the solitude has become stifling and I've drank myself to sleep. I'm not drinking to the point of having a hangover the following morning, only enough to help me fall asleep. Janice still pesters me to sit down with her so we can talk about her affair, but even saying the words "talk about my wife's affair" makes me sick to my stomach. I've only said them once, to Kate of all people, but she was incredibly helpful. Just having her to talk to has made this process much more bearable.

Kate and I have worked together on Evan's case three times in the last two weeks. We've had dinner twice. I asked her about Michael during our second dinner and though she tried to hide it, I could tell hearing his name made her sad. I didn't press her for details, but I felt terrible for talking to her about my marital issues when she clearly has her own. I can't imagine what would cause problems in a marriage when the couple is expecting their first child, especially when the wife is as amazing and caring as Kate. I can only assume Michael was a fool and did to Kate what Janice did to me.

"Ryan are you listening to me?" Kate's question snatches me out of my rapidly drifting thoughts.

"Yeah, sorry. I just have so much on my mind these days."

"I understand, but we need to focus. Evan's preliminary hearing is tomorrow and Bart is not going to go easy on us."

"What is wrong with that guy? It's like he wants to punish the whole world."

"Bart is a great attorney. He definitely makes the least deals out of all of the ADAs, but he's not going to prosecute someone unless he believes the person is guilty."

I study Kate in confusion. Surely she can't believe what she just said. "Kate, I have to say I disagree with you on this. I sat down with Bart. He knows Evan had a brain tumor. He knows the tumor's size and location on the brain were severe enough to cause blackouts. He knows a tumor of that size would leave a person in immeasurable pain. He saw the evidence, yet he insists on twisting the facts to make it seem as though Evan was drunk and let his daughter drown."

"Or maybe you're twisting the facts to make it seem as though Evan is innocent."

Again, I stare at Kate. I have no idea how she could believe any of what she just said. "Kate, if you believe Bart is right why did you agree to help me on this case?"

"I never said I thought Bart was right. I'm trying to get you to focus on the merits of the case instead of Bart. The judge doesn't need to hear your speculation about Bart tomorrow. He's going to want you to present a case as to why there is no probable cause for the charges. How are you going to defend Evan? He does have a history of drinking. His wife is going to testify that his drinking has been out of control for quite some time. How are you going to show Evan was sober when no one, not even our client, knows with absolute certainty what happened between the time Lisa Reynolds left for work, and when she returned?"

I finally understand why Thomas is so pissed at Michael for stealing Kate away. She's compassionate and probably the most emotional attorney I've ever seen, but she can turn all of that off and focus on the facts of the case.

"What do you suggest?"

"Well, for starters, we need to introduce the blood test results that show Evan had no alcohol in his system when he was initially arrested."

"I already tried that angle with Bart," I point out. "His counter was that several hours had passed and Evan's body had time to metabolize the alcohol, so the blood test means nothing."

"First, Bart is not a doctor," Kate countered. "He is only spitting out what he learned from interviewing potential expert witnesses. Those witnesses are paid by the state. I guarantee you we can find a witness to discredit their witness. Second, this is not a trial. This is a preliminary hearing. Bart has to prove he has enough evidence to justify the charges. We have to challenge said evidence."

"How can we challenge when we know Evan was home alone with his daughter when she died?"

"Do we know that? We know what the assumptions are. If Evan has no recollection of that morning, the timeline is solely based on Lisa Reynolds' testimony."

I blanch at the suggestion. I don't like what I'm hearing, but Kate has a point. I've been going at this all wrong. "I'll see if I can dig up anything to challenge Lisa's timeline."

"That's a good place to start. While you work on that, I'm going to dig into her past a little. I have a private investigator that I can call."

"I can just use one from the PD's office."

Kate laughed at my suggestion. "No offense Ryan, but I worked with those in-house guys for years. Trust me when I tell you Higgins is much better."

"Higgins? Isn't that the guy who worked on the Carrington case?"

"Yes. He actually did quite a bit of freelance work for Thomas over the years. Michael put an end to that though."

"Oh really. How so?"

"You know my husband. When he wants something from someone, he does whatever it takes to get it."

I didn't quite understand what Kate meant. I don't know her husband well, and what I know of him doesn't encourage me to dig deeper. I simply shrug the remark off. "I'm gonna get going. We have a lot of ground to cover today."

"Yes we do. Oh, and Ryan."

"Yes?"

"Don't expect to win this hearing tomorrow. Bart has probable cause."

"Then why the hell didn't we waive?"

"Because we need to see his hand. Bart is a decent attorney, but he's not great at subtlety. He often plays his cards too quickly. This hearing will give us a jump on discovery."

I smile and nod as I walk out the door. Kate is a far better strategist than I ever realized. Working with her is going to be much better than working with her husband.

***

"All rise. The honorable Judge Walter Roberts now presiding."

Going before Judge Roberts is always a delicate dance. You never know what type of mood he's going to be in. Rumor has it, he drinks most of his meals, but he's never appeared to be under the influence when I've appeared before him, except today. Today, the Judge's normally clear and alert eyes are red and glassy. His robe is disheveled. I don't even understand how one can be disheveled in a big black robe, but Judge Roberts has managed. It's 9am and the judge is drunk as a skunk. I glance at Kate for direction, but she keeps her eyes straight ahead. I glance back at the judge, and notice he's lost a considerable amount of weight since I last appeared before him. That was only two months ago, an appeal on a misdemeanor charge which we lost, but he's lost at least 20 pounds since then. I wonder for a moment why this man is still allowed to sit on the bench, and the answer comes quickly. Judges in the great state of North Carolina are allowed to serve on the bench until the age of 72. Judge Roberts will reach his mandatory retirement age next week. The judge has served on the bench in Mecklenburg County since he won his first election 40 years ago. 32 seems like a young age to become a judge. I'm only five years younger and I in no way believe I am ready for such an important role. In our state however, one must only graduate law school and pass the bar to become a judge. There is no age requirement or minimum number of years one has to actually practice the law. I suspect this is one of the main reasons none of the lawyers have made much of a fuss about Judge Roberts' alleged drinking. Though his behavior has been bizarre, his rulings have been fair. No one wants to risk losing a veteran judge with a long legacy of fair and accurate rulings when the standards are so low for replacements. All over the state we are seeing skilled judges, that have served the bench honorably, lose elections. Young inexperienced candidates with the gift of gab or familiar last names are winning by a landslide because the general public does not know or understand that the eligibility requirements to run for judge are minimal. Gubernatorial appointments haven't always been the best replacements either. The most recent appointment was two years ago, a 28 year old from a family whose political connections run just as deep if not deeper than their pockets. At this point though, no matter how much we all dread it, Judge Roberts will be forced to retire next week and the Governor will appoint a replacement to hold the seat until the next election.

"Good morning Mr. Winslow," Judge Roberts slurs from the bench as he looks down at Bart. "Are you ready to get started?"

"Yes sir."

"Good morning Ms. Young. Are you ready?"

"Yes sir," Kate replies with a strained smile. She's been Mrs. Ayers for a year now and Judge Roberts hasn't bothered to address her by her married name due to his disdain for her now deceased father-in-law. Kate knows better than to correct him, especially in his current state.

"Bring the defendant in."

The bailiff disappears for a moment, then returns with a shackled and still badly bruised Evan. The sight of him is difficult to stomach. It's difficult to believe one man can endure such pain and still get out of bed. Evan takes his place between Kate and me at the defense table. Within minutes I dread putting Evan through this. Bart's first witness is Lisa and she wastes no time painting Evan as a sloppy drunk whose best friend is Jack Daniels. Kate did a great job of forcing Lisa to admit she hadn't seen Evan drink for weeks prior to the accident during cross, but the damage was done. At the end of the hearing Judge Roberts ruled as expected, there is probable cause for Evan to be charged with murder. Although Kate previously told me this would be the outcome, I still cringed. Watching

Evan lose what little hope he had for life as his wife sat on the stand and testified against him, did something to me that I can't quite explain. One thing is for certain, I'll never be the same.

Chapter 14
Michael

It's been said that the most important people in a
criminal case are the twelve people that are inside of
the jury box. I agree with that statement, but I like to
include a thirteenth person, the judge. Judges have
played important roles within the community since
biblical days. They decide what the jury hears and what
they don't hear. They ultimately decide the fate of
defendants during the sentencing portion of trials. In
cases like the one I am currently working on, the sole
discretion as to whether or not a defendant sees the
inside of a prison is left to the judge. One would think
holding the ability to change the course of a person's
life is a responsibility only given to those mature
enough to understand the magnitude of their decision.
Well, the person that believes this would be wrong.

I got the news about the Governor's new appointments two weeks ago. Governor Jim Kasey was arguably one of the most popular men to hold the office of Governor in recent history. He served the State of North Carolina for a total of four terms. The rule is that Governors are only allowed to serve two consecutive four year terms, but there is nothing that bars them from returning to office after taking a break for at least one term. After serving his two consecutive terms, Governor Kasey took his required four year break while the Governor elected to serve after him crashed and burned. Like any skilled politician, Governor Kasey spent those four years with his ear to the ground. Rumor has it his eyes were on Washington, but when he was overlooked for Presidential cabinet positions, he turned his attention back to his home state. His approval rating remained very high amongst nearly every demographic across the state. Seeing an opportunity to win again, Governor Kasey threw his hat into the gubernatorial race for a third time and became the second Governor in North Carolina history to return to office after previously serving two consecutive terms. His record was impeccable over the first two terms, but the third term proved to be problematic for his approval rating. As the needs of the people of our state changed, Governor Kasey's opinions on important social issues did not. North Carolina was thrown into the national spotlight due to policies that were largely viewed as unconstitutional and discriminatory. The embarrassment to the state was eclipsed by the lost revenue after major organizations withdrew plans to do business in our state. I, like most Carolinians, believe Governor Kasey knew he did not stand a chance at ever winning another election. The writing was definitely on the wall, so it was no surprise when the Governor did not run for re-election. Even knowing all of this, I don't think anyone could have predicted what Governor Kasey would do next.

Governor Kasey, now unconcerned about his approval rating, held the responsibility to appoint two judges, one to serve as a District Court Judge to replace Judge Roberts and a Superior Court Judge to replace Judge Burr, a very qualified judge who was recently forced to resign after being diagnosed with brain cancer. The district seat was not nearly as big of an appointment because district court judges only serve four year terms.

As it stands, we are three years into the term. The newly appointed judge is going to have to run for re-election soon. The bigger issue lay with the appointee that will replace Judge Burr. Superior Court Judges serve eight year terms. There are five years remaining in Judge Burr's current term. This newly appointed Judge will be presiding over thousands of cases during those five years. The very first of which will be the case of the State of North Carolina v. Ron Edahl.

As I watch newly appointed Judge Constance Lewis slowly strut into the courtroom with an air of superiority only an entitled person with little regard for issues outside of their own would, I glance over at McMurray. I now understand why he was so pissed when he called me. He thinks I somehow helped Ron get this case assigned to Judge Lewis. There are several reasons as to why I would not take part in such a conspiracy. The biggest reason is that the risk is too great. I know nothing of the 27 year old who looks like she belongs on a Panthers' sideline rather than on the bench. I tried to dig into her past, but the only information I could find was mostly generic. She graduated law school and passed the bar last year. She worked for a small boutique firm handling mostly misdemeanor cases. How she ever made her way onto the Governor's radar to even be considered for judgeship is a mystery. Nonetheless, here she is wearing a façade of confidence attempting to preside over her first felony case. She has no previous rulings that could help me estimate how she might rule today. I'm scared shitless, yet my client seems cooler than ice in the winter.

I lean over and whisper in Ron's ear. "Did you do anything that could land either of us in jail to make this happen?"

"I told you not to worry," Ron whispers back.

I'm not convinced, but there is nothing I can do at this point. I brace myself for the most unconventional trial court arraignment I've ever experienced.

"Your Honor," McMurray begins, "if it pleases the court, I'd like to make a suggestion here."

I'm instantly stunned to silence. McMurray would never breach protocol with an experienced judge. He's purposely exploiting Judge Lewis' inexperience.

Something inside of me tells me this little stunt is going to backfire. I watch in perfect stillness.

"Your Honor, with this being your first case, and due to the complications of this case, I would like to respectfully ask you to recuse yourself. I assure you I mean no disrespect with this request, it's just that I believe the defense counsel and the defendant have conspired to have this case assigned to you in hopes of receiving leniency from this court."

I hold my breath waiting for Judge Lewis to respond. When she finally speaks, it takes everything in me to keep a straight face.

"Mr. McMurray, do you have any evidence to support your claim of judicial misconduct by defense counsel?"

"No ma'am, I do not. I believe this to be true based on the Defense Counsel's character and previous actions Your Honor."

"Mr. McMurray I'm sure you are aware this courtroom operates based on facts presented as evidence, not suspicions and unsubstantiated allegations. Without any evidence to support your claim and with great exception being taken at your unspoken accusation that

I somehow am incapable of doing my job of judging this case based solely on the letter of the law, I am going to deny your request and move forward with why we are here today."

The heat radiating from McMurray makes its way to the defense table. I stand there feeling the invisible arrows being aimed directly for my heart as Judge Lewis starts the arraignment. I try not to, but the entire time she talks, I study her lips. I'm not watching to actually hear and understand her words, instead I'm soaking in her appearance. Everything about the judge screams fish out of water. Her full lips are colored by a dark red lipstick with some sort of shimmer. They look completely different from anything I've ever seen Kate wear. I attribute this to the age difference. Judge Lewis' hair is long and full. Just the sight of it makes me want to reach out and run my fingers through it. I imagine the feel of it flowing through my fingers. I focus in on her eyes. They are large and brown with a look of absolute terror. Despite her confident words, I can see through her tough guy routine. She's actually frightened and McMurray's assumption of her inability to accurately judge this trial is spot on.

"How does the defendant plead?" Judge Lewis' question helps me to focus and snap out of the trance her beauty has me under.

Ron speaks loud and clear. "I plead guilty Your Honor."

There are gasps from the gallery and for the first time I turn around to see the spectators have filled every available seat. I glance around the crowd and spot my wife sitting in a corner. She averts her gaze ruining any chance at making eye contact, but her presence means more to me than she knows. I continue scanning the crowd and spot Tanya sitting on the opposite side of the room. She's sitting on the prosecution's side with her arm around a woman who's covering her face with her hands. I can tell by the rise and fall of the woman's shoulders that she's crying. Unlike Kate, Tanya is staring straight at me wearing a look that can kill.

Judge Lewis bangs her gavel demanding silence in the courtroom. I hear a couple clicks of cameras and silently cringe realizing the media is here. The vultures are greedily looking for ways to spin this case into the most sensational cover story possible. I quickly try to minimize future damage to my case.

"Your Honor, my client is ready for sentencing."

"I object Your Honor," McMurray yells. "The State needs time to properly prepare. There are aggravating factors the State would like you to consider before sentencing the defendant."

"The defense is ready to present mitigating factors Your Honor. We can proceed immediately."

"This is highly irregular Your Honor. Again, the defense is attempting to exploit your inexperience."

And does it. That is the sentence that pushes Judge Lewis over the edge. She bangs her gavel again and shoots daggers at McMurray as she speaks.

"You've been warned Mr. McMurray. Making unsubstantiated allegations and innuendo regarding my judgement will not be tolerated. I won't warn you again. Now...in the interest of expediency and fairness to all, we will recess until 1pm this afternoon. At which time both the state and defense will be given an opportunity to present their factors...."

"Your Honor, that is hardly enough..."

Judge Lewis bangs her gavel hard again. "Mr. McMurray you seem to be so concerned with my ability to do my job that you are forgetting your role in the judicial process. This is my courtroom. When I speak, you listen. Interrupting me while I am rendering a decision is unacceptable and unprofessional. Interrupt me again and I will hold you in contempt. Court is adjourned until 1pm," Judge Lewis says as she bangs her gavel and angrily stands and leaves the courtroom.

McMurray clearly unglued by his anger gathers his paperwork and also storms out of the courtroom. Reporters rush to ask him questions, but he pushes them all out of the way as he charges full speed ahead. I lean over and whisper to Ron.

"Don't say a word to anyone. Don't make eye contact, just keep your head down and get out of here without incident."

I turn and begin leaving the courtroom when I hear Ron's voice.

"I want to publicly apologize to the family of Khalil Jeffries. That morning I was awakened by the screams of my one and only child." Ron pauses and begins to cry. He sobs for a moment and I use the break to get back to him. Once at his side, I try to put an end to the interview with the over anxious reporter holding the microphone in my client's face.

"My client is still grieving for his daughter. Please, allow us the opportunity to present a full statement at a later date." I tug at Ron's arm attempting to get him to leave the courtroom. Ron resists for a moment before starting to slowly walk out of the courtroom. The entire time his head is held down as he mumbles, "I didn't mean it. I thought he was hurting her."

I rush Ron away from the courthouse and towards my car. Once we are safely away from the microphones and cameras of the vultures that call themselves journalists, I lay into Ron like a mad man.

"What the hell was that? Do you want to go to jail?"

Ron wipes the tears from his face and actually smiles at me. "Do you think the judge will see the footage on the news before we reconvene at 1?"

I shake my head in disgust. Who is this man? The Ron I know is kind and gentle. He couldn't hurt a fly. This cold calculating person that just cried at the drop of a hat is a stranger to me.

"Ron, what's going on here? I've known you most of my life and none of this makes any sense."

"Michael, I made a mistake that morning. I thought that son of a bitch was raping my daughter. If you were a parent, you'd understand."

"But he wasn't raping her. He was her boyfriend. You killed an innocent kid and not to mention your own daughter. How can you be so cold about this?"

"I'm not cold. I'll have to live with what I did for the rest of my life, but I don't deserve to go to prison. Michelle was an accident. I'll never forgive myself for hurting her, but that bastard was in *my* house having sex with *my* daughter! No matter how you look at it, that was a violation. I'm not sorry he's dead. Any dad who says he wouldn't have tried to do the same thing I did is a liar."

"But why the Dr. Jekyll and Mr. Hyde act? What was that back there?"

Ron looks straight at me as a wide sadistic grin spreads across his face. "I did some digging on Judge Lewis. She's smart, but nowhere near prepared to handle this trial. She was heard saying she didn't think I should be facing charges at all. Plus, get this," Ron says as he laughs, "she's never been on television before. She was anxious to see how she was going to look. I'm sure she's going to watch the midday newscast. No way she'll make me serve any actual time in prison after watching me cry and mumble like an idiot."

I pull my car to a screeching halt causing the driver behind me to lay on his horn. We're sitting in the middle of traffic and I don't care. I turn to face Ron. "You mean to tell me you've been spying on a Superior Court Judge? You planned all of this and used me as a pawn! You put me, my firm, and my family in jeopardy because as you said, the bastard deserved it?"

"Calm down. I assured you this would not come back to you."

"Bullshit Ron! You can't do something like this without it coming back to bite me in the ass. I've worked too damn hard to let you drag me down on some bullshit conspiracy charge!"

"Watch your tone with me. I've known you since before you knew your head from your ass. I spent more time trying to mold you into a man than your lazy self-centered parents ever did."

The remark about my parents is the final straw. I turn away from Ron and start driving again. Ron starts speaking, but I'm so angry I can't hear anything he's saying. I'm using every ounce of self-restraint I have to keep myself in line so that I don't beat the living shit out of Ron. Listening to this dark, twisted side of him is like a child learning there is no Santa Claus, like learning Superman is just Clark Kent with a bunch of studio magic. In short, my idol is a disgusting asshole and as soon as this case is over, I'll never speak to him again.

***

The Judge's Ruling

The courtroom is filled to capacity as everyone holds their breath in anticipation of the judge's ruling. Judge Lewis takes her time reviewing the papers in front of her as we all wait. I'm annoyed because she clearly knows what's on the pages, but she's forcing all of us to wait as though we're all on an episode of one of those wretched day time television shows. I find myself hoping she throws the book at Ron. I know he's my client, but he should not be allowed to murder two people in cold blood, then play the system into letting him off easy. Ron planned all of this, including rushing the proceedings before the general public began protesting. While I typically applaud anyone who is able to outsmart the system, this case makes me sick to my stomach. Ron is a horrible person, and standing next to him is making my blood boil.

"This is a very interesting case," Judge Lewis begins. "On the one hand, we have two teenagers whose lives have been cut short. On the other hand, we have a father who genuinely believed his daughter's life was in danger. After listening to the testimonies from Khalil Jeffries' mother as well as the witnesses presented by the defense, I find that while this loss of life is absolutely heartbreaking, Mr. Edahl faced an impossible situation that fatal morning when he heard screams coming from his daughter's bedroom. There is nothing a father won't do when an intruder enters his home and begins to rape his only daughter. Mr. Edahl, I offer you my condolences on the loss of your daughter and I salute you for your willingness to take responsibility for your role in her death. With that being said, on count one, murder in the second degree for the death of Michelle Edahl, I am rejecting your guilty plea and dismissing the charge against you."

Instantly the court erupts in yelling and commotion. There are all sorts of hateful words being yelled at Ron. Judge Lewis bangs her gavel.

"Quiet, or I'll clear this courtroom!"

It takes a moment, but everyone settles down and waits for the judge to continue.

"As it pertains to the second victim, I am torn. Khalil Jeffries was a promising young football star. By all accounts, this young man had a very bright future ahead of him. I am deeply saddened by the loss of a talented and thoughtful young man. To the Jeffries family, please accept this court's sincere condolences for your loss. Nothing this court does will bring your son back to you, and for that our thoughts and prayers will be with your family as you mourn the loss of a special young man." Judge Lewis pauses and takes a long cleansing breath before continuing. Anticipation hangs in the air like a buzzard hovering over his prey waiting for it to take its last breath.

"Mr. Edahl," Judge Lewis continues, "there were several mitigating factors considered in reaching an appropriate sentence for your crime. This crime was committed under duress, and although you acted in a moment of extreme concern for the safety of your daughter, you have no history of violence towards anyone. By all accounts, you are a man of good moral character that provides substantial support to your community. You are the sole provider for your family and employ a large number of people in the city of Charlotte as well as Mecklenburg County at large. While you admitted wrong doing very early in this process, it is the belief of this court that you are an asset to this community and show no signs of causing bodily harm to anyone else in the future. With that in mind, this court sentences you to a suspended sentence of 18 months and five years of supervised probation. If you violate probation in any way your 18 month sentence will be...."

Before the judge can finish her sentence, the room erupts into massive chaos as a member of Khalil Jeffries family leaps over the banister and directly onto Ron knocking him to the ground. My breathing becomes rapid and shallow as my brain tries to process what's unfolding around me. I want to move away from the commotion but I am glued to the floor. I tell myself to run... retreat... find safety, but my chest is tightening and my body will not cooperate. I feel a stinging sensation in my chest as my lungs burn for air. Sweat begins to race down my face. I hear the sound of my internal voice begging me to breathe, to move away from the fight on the floor in front of me. I'm jostled a bit as deputies try to pry the grief-stricken man away from Ron. All at once, as quickly as it began, my body switches from frantic to still. It's like I'm locked deep within myself with my senses on high alert, but my brain is slowly drifting into an alluring state of rest. Rest would be a welcomed relief right now. I could use just a moment of sweet peace to escape the scene that is still unfolding before me. Just as I feel my eye lids begin to lower under the heavy weight of breathless fatigue, someone pulls me hard. The tug breaks my trance and I turn to see Kate. Her lips are moving, but none of what she is saying registers for me. Suddenly air rushes into my lungs and I lean over coughing and gasping for air. The sounds around me begin to filter in although I still can't quite place where everything is coming from. I feel more moisture run down my face and realize it isn't sweat. I'm crying. Fear has gripped me and I can't focus enough to figure out how to get out of the courtroom. Kate pulls me again and this time my feet move toward her. Within moments, Kate has pulled me out into the hallway. She holds my face in her hands and for the first time I notice she's crying too.

"Breathe baby. It's okay. Just focus on breathing."

I follow Kate's commands as the weight of what just happened begins to set in. As a man of great pride in my reputation, I have no clue how to move forward.

Chapter 15
Ryan

I've been calling Kate all morning with no response. Walking past the conference room at the office, I finally realize why. As Thomas and the other associates at the PD's office watch in a mixture of disbelief and delight, I feel my stomach leap into my throat as the reporter's words float from the wall mounted television and into the hallway.

"Pandemonium broke out in a Charlotte courtroom today as Raymond Jeffries, father of Khalil Jeffries, attacked the man that plead guilty to killing his son. Khalil Jeffries was just seventeen years old when his life was cut short by Ron Edahl, a prominent local businessman, who at the time of the attack, believed Jeffries was sexually assaulting his daughter. Violence erupted after newly appointed Judge Constance Lewis announced Ron Edahl

will not spend a single day behind bars for the crime. That's when Raymond Jeffries snapped and began to physically attack Mr. Edahl. It took several Sheriff's deputies to separate the two men. At the center of it all was Mr. Edahl's attorney Michael Ayers. A man, who just a year ago was wounded when gunshots were fired inside of the courtroom. It appears Mr. Ayers was very shaken up during today's incident. It is unclear if Mr. Ayers suffered any injuries or whether or not Raymond Jeffries will face charges for today's attack. Ron Edahl was transported to Carolina Medical Center. No word yet on the extent of his injuries. We'll bring you more on this story as it develops."

I stand in total shock as some of my colleagues hint that Michael and Ron both got what they deserved. I'm unable to move as they begin filing out of the conference room. I don't know if I'll ever understand how humans can be so callous to suffering. They disperse with smiles on their faces after watching a man being beaten and another completely fall apart. Who are these people?

Thomas is the last to leave and I know as soon as he lays eyes on me that he's pissed. "Mr. Du Bois, I need to see you in my office right away."

I don't bother responding. I follow Thomas into his office and shut the door behind me. It doesn't take a genius to recognize this conversation needs to stay between the two of us. Lawyers love gossip. They won't get any at my expense.

"You and I both know why you're in here. I have the paperwork drawn up. You just need to sign and clean out your desk."

"Wait....what? You're firing me?"

"What did you think would happen when you involved Ayers & Ayers in our case?"

"You said yourself this case would have normally gone to Kate. Why should you care that she's agreed to help? She's a great attorney with a passion for the innocent. Evan needs her."

"We both know Kate wasn't your choice. Your hero turned you down. That fact aside, you broke protocol by seeking outside counsel without prior approval. That's my only concern."

"My hero? Concern? Bullshit! You weren't concerned when you stuck a guy with no felony trial experience on a case that clearly needed a more experienced attorney."

"What did you just say to me?"

"You heard me! You set me up from the beginning. You've barely said more than a few words to me then suddenly I'm your go to guy for a murder case? You think I'm stupid! That's why you put me on the case. You never expected me to find the connection between Tanya and Lisa Reynolds!"

"You're right about one thing, I did set you up. I set you up to springboard your career. You've been here too long to shy away from the tough cases. Why did you become a lawyer in the first place if you weren't prepared to handle cases?"

"Don't try to make this about me! You know damn well I needed more experience. You set Evan up for failure and used Tanya to help you! Where's your adequate counsel mug now?"

"What the hell are you accusing me of?"

"A gross misuse of your office for starters, and sleeping with someone under your direction supervision. I wonder how your faithful supporters will feel when they find out they voted for an asshole who sleeps with his employees and manipulates the defense of clients he's not fond of."

"Tanya is an ex-employee. And whether or not I'm sleeping with her has nothing to do with my job or yours. You're nothing more than a second rate attorney who should be grateful I've kept you around this long. Public perception is important. Let's not forget how angry the black community is about your ineffective counsel last year. Who stepped in to save you then?"

"You didn't step in to save anything. You sat your self-righteous ass right in this office and let me be crucified on the news."

Thomas actually begins to laugh. This isn't a laugh I've ever heard come from him. It's a sinister sound that tells me exactly what he thinks of everything I'm saying. I don't bother waiting to hear what he'll say next. I know when I'm being played for a fool. I storm out of the office and slam the door behind me. Thomas thinks firing me is punishment, but he just freed me. Evan Reynolds is now going to get the representation he deserves without the restraints of the public defender's office.

It's been five hours since I stormed out of Thomas' office, and out of the 4th Street public defender's office forever. For the second time since learning of Janice's affair I'm crying. Deep pools of sadness are pouring from my eyes as I sit in the dark nursing a glass of Jack and Coke. This is my new reality. My wife cheated on me, I'm a part time father, and now I'm unemployed. I don't understand how my life took such a steep dive in just a few weeks. My ringing cell phone interrupts my pity party.

"Hello."

"Hey Ryan, it's Kate. I'm sorry it took me so long to get back to you. It's been a crazy day. I'm sure you've seen the news."

"Yes. How's Michael?"

"He's getting there. Look, I don't want to seem crass, but we're on a tight time crunch. With all that's going on, we're gonna need a sharp mind at the office. We need to hire someone we can trust, and I suggested to Michael that you are that person. I know my husband wasn't the nicest to you when you met with him, but he was under a lot of stress that day. Ron Edahl was like a second father to him. That doesn't excuse his behavior, but I want you to know he wasn't quite himself. If you accept our offer, I'll make sure your salary compensates you for that meeting and some of the future ones I'm sure you'll have to endure. You haven't really seen it, but I'm sure you've heard rumors about my passionate side as well. Michael and I can both be intense. We want to make sure you know and understand this coming in."

"It's fine. Working at Ayers & Ayers has to be better than working at the public defender's office," I say cutting her off with more enthusiasm than I intend to show. "I'll be there in the morning. Thomas fired me today, so I can start immediately."

"Thomas fired you?"

"Yes. I'd like to explain in person if that's okay."

"You don't have to. I know Thomas. He fired you for coming to us for help. I swear, that man has a great legal mind, but he has to be one of the most egotistical people alive. And that's saying a lot coming from someone married to a man that could make a serious run for that title."

"You get no argument from me on that one."

Kate sighs heavily into the phone. I can hear the tension in her breath. I meant to make her laugh with my comment. I didn't intend to make her feel worse.

"I'm sorry," I quickly stammer. "I was just trying to make the conversation a little lighter."

"Oh no, it's not that. It's just that we are really going to have our hands full over the next few weeks and Evan deserves to have focused defense counsel."

"You're right. It's going to be tough, but we can handle it. Evan will not be convicted. I can promise you that."

***

I'm standing on the street staring up at the house that I once called home. Talking to Kate and hearing her concern for Michael made me miss my wife. I'm still hurt, and afraid, but most of all I'm angry. I don't understand how Janice could have ruined everything we have worked so hard to build. I see movement in a window upstairs and my eyes dart quickly enough to see Janice looking out of our bedroom window. She vanishes almost immediately, but I'm sure she saw me. At this hour Kaitlin is asleep, which is probably best, because I want time to talk without interruption. I'm ready to let Janice explain. I don't know if I'll be able to forgive her, but at least I'm ready to hear the whole story. That's a step in the right direction.

It only takes a moment for Janice to open the front door. She doesn't come down to talk to me. Instead, she stands with her oversized cardigan wrapped tightly around her as she waits for me to make the next move. I can tell in her demeanor she is not the same woman that followed me out of the house begging me to forgive her. Janice is pissed. The idea that she has the nerve to be angry with me makes my own emotions start to waiver. I came here to hear her out, not start a fight. I'm still a few drinks past sober which is why I took an Uber here instead of driving. I know I'm not the best person to converse with when I'm tipsy so I take a few calming breaths before I begin to walk towards the house. I urge my heart and brain to both work with me so that I can take in everything Janice has to say without saying something that will trigger an argument. I inwardly acknowledge that I have no clue how I'm going to react when Janice tells me everything, and that scares the shit out of me.

Chapter 16
Michael

It's been two days since Ron escaped prison time and I had a panic attack in the courtroom. Kate has been by my side nearly every moment, but today is the day we have to get back to the real world. I'd be lying if I said I was ready. I'm not. And the fact of the matter is, I'm not sure if I'll ever be ready to return to the courtroom. The attack on Ron brought feelings to the surface that I've never dealt with or even acknowledged. I've awakened in a cold sweat for the past two nights. Both nights I had vivid dreams of John Kiplinger standing over me aiming a gun straight at my face. Kate thinks I need a therapist. I disagree. What I really need to do is stop practicing criminal law. Criminal law has done nothing but bring me grief since my very first case. Every time I work a criminal case someone dies, a guilty defendant escapes jail time, or mayhem erupts in the courtroom. I've made more than my fair share of enemies practicing criminal law. That's enough for any responsible husband and father-to-be to change his profession. I won't leave Kate and our son to mourn my untimely passing all because I was too arrogant to see the signs and walk away while I still could. No. Ron Edahl will be my final violent criminal case. Going forward, the closest I'll go to criminal cases will be simple white collar crimes where the criminals are money hungry business men and women. I'll pick my cases much more carefully and turn away anyone with any type of violence in their past. I'll handle civil litigation...anything that keeps me away from felony murder trials.

Kate walks into our bedroom wearing a short silk robe that barely covers anything now that our son is stretching her belly. The look in her eye tells me I am in for a treat I have not had the pleasure of enjoying since she moved out of our home.

"Mike, work is going to be tough today. You're still all over the news and reporters have been hanging out around the office."

My face hardens. "Why would you come in here dressed like that, looking like that...just to tell me work is going to be tough?"

"Well, that's not all I came to say, but I figured I should get the bad news out of the way first."

"So what's the good news?" I asked with an arched brow.

"The good news is I've forgiven you. I see how I made a mountain out of a molehill." Kate stops talking as she slowly begins to untie her robe. She stares up at me seductively as the robe falls open revealing her beautiful body. My body responds instantly. She takes another step closer to me.

"Since you were the one that blew things out of proportion, shouldn't I be doing the forgiving?" I ask teasingly.

"You're right," Kate says as she closes the distance between us. "Do you forgive me?"

"I'm not sure. You really wounded me," I say mockingly as a wicked smile spreads across my face. "How far are you willing to go to make it up to me?"

"Well, first I am going to help you forget all about work. Then, I'm going to help you release all of that pent-up stress."

***

Four hours later, Kate and I walk into the office without any fanfare. My guess is that the press gave up when we didn't arrive at our normal time, because we didn't spot a single reporter. Kate was right about one thing, I needed the hours of love making to recover from the stress of the previous weeks. I feel like a new man, ready to get his life and business back on track. Kate phoned ahead and notified the staff we'd be having a mandatory meeting during lunch.

We walked into the conference room to find the eyes of all our associates on us. Well more accurately, it felt as though everyone was staring directly at me, like they wanted to see if I was going to snap. I surveyed the room looking each of them in the eye. I stopped briefly on Ryan Du Bois. Kate mentioned hiring him, but it was still a little odd seeing him here. I never thought he was much of an attorney, but my wife tells me he has potential. I continue perusing the crowd until my eyes reach Tanya. I'm shocked she had the nerve to show up. I lean in and whisper in Kate's ear.

"What is Tanya doing here?"

"I haven't been here to fire her, remember?" she whispers back.

"Fine. I want to do it anyway. Go ahead and start the meeting and I'll take care of her."

"No Michael, let's do it together after the meeting."

"Like hell! I'm not going to let her stay here to gather more information to use against us."

Kate leans back and examines my eyes. I can tell she realizes I'm serious. She turns to face the crowd of eyes staring at us. "Thank you for waiting everyone. We appreciate all of your loyalty and support. We want you guys to go ahead and help yourself to lunch. If you take a seat, the staff from Morrison's Cafeteria will come and serve you. Michael and I will give you a chance to eat before we get the meeting started. Enjoy your lunch."

Everyone takes their seat and the efficient staff from Morrison's begins bringing plates to the tables. Kate smiles as she looks out at our employees. Marrying her and bringing her on board as a full partner is one of the best decisions I've ever made. Kate is the epitome of grace and has the unique ability to control a crowd without coming across as controlling. I don't have half of the tact she has. Just as everyone gets seated, Kate walks over to Tanya and speaks softly in her ear. Tanya shoots a hateful glance in my direction before following Kate towards me. Both ladies walk past me leaving the room without looking in my direction. I follow behind them anxious to get behind closed doors so I can say what I really want to say to Tanya.

Once we are safely behind the closed doors of Kate's office I turn to Tanya, but Kate grabs my arm before I can open my mouth. I look at her and quickly relent. She doesn't have to speak for me to understand what she is saying.

"Tanya," Kate begins, "Michael and I want to thank you for your service to Ayers & Ayers, but as of this moment, your position is no longer needed. We will not provide a severance package."

"Like hell you won't! I'll leave, but I'm not leaving empty handed."

"What did you just say?" My anger comes out stronger than I intend.

"You heard me. Y'all aren't just gonna use me then leave me unemployed. You know damn well I just closed on my house."

"Tanya, your personal finances are not the concern of Ayers & Ayers. We payed you well during your time here, but we have decided to eliminate your position."

"Why, because I'm black?" Tanya asks with that neck roll she pulls out every time she hears something she doesn't like.

"Race has nothing to do with this," Kate adds while still maintaining her professional demeanor. "You are a legal secretary. We need a lawyer who has already passed the bar to help with some of our more challenging cases and the only way to fit a new associate into the budget is to eliminate one of the legal secretaries."

"You still haven't told me why me. I'm the only *black* legal secretary, so I guess I was the obvious choice. You can just throw me out when you feel like it, huh? Is that how Ayers & Ayers views its black employees, like expendables?"

"We made the decision based on education, not race which would be highly illegal, and we resent your accusation. You are one of the highest paid secretaries, yet you have the least amount of education. It is in the best interest of the firm to eliminate your position. Now, if you'll excuse us, we'll have your belongings boxed up and mailed to you. Michael and I need to get back to the meeting."

"No one will be boxing up anything of mine. I brought my stuff in and I will be taking it out." Tanya stood and opened the door only to find security standing there waiting for her.

I turn to smile at my beautiful and equally intelligent wife. She anticipated Tanya's outburst and put a plan in place for it. I lean over and kiss my wife passionately. I didn't know my sweet Kate had it in her to be so calculating and I'm even more attracted to her now that I've seen this side.

Chapter 17
Ryan

Janice and I sit in the den surrounded by darkness except for the light coming from the small table lamp on the end table. I want it this way. I don't want her to be able to see my face just in case an errant tear escapes from me. Drinking before I came over was a very bad idea. I can't always keep my emotions in check when I'm drinking and depending on what Janice says I need to be in control.

"I need to get a cup of coffee before you start," I announce as I get up and start walking towards the kitchen without waiting for her to respond. Before the words left my mouth, I knew she wasn't going to stop me, but I wasn't expecting her to follow me. Janice takes a seat at a stool at the breakfast bar while I start the Keurig. I try not to look at her, but her voice shocks me. I didn't expect her to start talking in here where the light can betray me and reveal every emotion as it passes over my face.

"I never slept with him. I swear Ryan. I would never let it get that far."

"Then what *did* you do? Because I heard you say you'd been screwing your boss," I say with enough venom to kill a thousand people and I instantly know this was a bad idea. I'm still too hurt, too raw for this conversation. I shouldn't have come here.

Janice does not react to my comment. "It started with extra accolades about my work. Clifton knew I was a little self-conscious about some of my designs after that big client ripped me to shreds last year. I thought he was just being nice because he knew I was a good employee. Then he started asking me to lunch. We would talk about work. Strictly work. He never said anything remotely close to flirting for the first couple of months. I didn't see it coming. But when he went to Europe two months ago, I realized I missed him more than I should have. I felt lonely without him and that's when I realized I'd started to develop feelings for him.

I thought it was one sided so I tried to make them go away on my own. I figured it was harmless. I thought it was like a school girl's crush, but when he came back he told me he'd spent more time than he cared to admit thinking about me while he was away. He apologized for crossing the line. He said the only reason he told me was because he didn't think we should spend so much time together anymore, and he didn't want me to think I'd done anything wrong."

"So if that's all it was, why did you say you'd been seeing him?" I ask feeling even more hurt than when I thought she was just screwing the guy.

"Because it didn't end there. I had lunch with him nearly every day knowing we had feelings for each other, then we had dinner. I felt terrible when I came home and knew I had to stop before things went too far."

"When did you have dinner with him?"

"The night I told you we had an afterhours open house."

I hang my head as the pain shoots through my heart causing the first few tears to fall. My wife had an affair and I was completely clueless. My mind travels back to the day she called me and said she forgot to tell me about the open house. She sounded perfectly normal. My thoughts race back through the conversation, analyzing the tone and pace of her speech. There was nothing... nothing to indicate my wife was lying. How the hell can I ever trust her after knowing how easy it was for her to lie to me? I want to speak, to say something...anything, but the words refuse to come out.

"Ryan, I'm sorry. I know I could have just ended it and not said anything but I felt too guilty. I felt like you deserved to know what I did. I swear on my life, on our daughter's life that I never slept with him. I never even kissed him, but I was still wrong and the guilt was eating me alive. I had to tell you."

"So you ripped my heart out and stepped all over it just to make yourself feel better?" The tears are flowing now, completely unchecked.

"I didn't want to hurt you Ryan, but you've been so good to me. I had to be honest with you. I ended it, but that wasn't enough. I don't want to be one of those women that thinks it's okay to cheat as long as she can get away with it. I let myself fall into something that I didn't see coming and I got out. I don't want to be with Clifton or any other man. I want to be with you."

"Then why did you fall for him?"

"I didn't fall for him. I started to develop feelings...yes, but I don't love him. I never loved him. You're the only man I'll ever love."

"Feelings, huh? Why didn't you sleep with him then? You said you wanted to sleep with me when you started developing feelings for me. And don't start lying to me now. Since you're telling me everything, don't hold back on this."

"It wasn't like that. I wanted his attention and I enjoyed his mind. We're passionate about the same things. He's the only person that I could talk to about my work that would match my enthusiasm with his own. When you come home all we talk about is Kaitlin and your job. No one asks me how my day went. No one cared about my job. Clifton was there and he cared about how I felt about my work. He helped me work through creative struggles. He saw me at a time when I felt like everyone else was seeing through me, like I wasn't even there."

My eyes shoot up to meet hers. "Are you actually blaming this on me? Are you saying I ignored you?"

"No! Ryan, you asked me a question. You asked me to be honest with you. I'm trying to do that. Clifton filled a space that I didn't even realize was empty."

"And I couldn't have filled it? You couldn't have come to me?"

"Ryan, how could I come to you when I didn't even know there was a problem? My life here is all about you and Kaitlin. I was losing myself and Clifton helped me to see that. It was nice to be asked about my work. It was nice to be treated like what I did mattered."

My anger rushes out of me like molten lava flowing from a long inactive volcano. "Bullshit! I'm not buying this poor little ignored me routine you're trying to sell. Clifton is rich and you looked at him and saw dollar signs. You threw our marriage away because you wanted to. You're not gonna turn this shit around on me!"

"So now I'm a whore that jumps on the first rich penis she sees?"

"I thought you said you didn't sleep with him!" I yell as I throw my coffee cup still full of coffee at the kitchen wall. I watch the dark brown liquid drip down the white subway tiles with a small hint of satisfaction. Janice doesn't even flinch.

"I didn't sleep with him! Stop twisting my words and listen to me! You're proving my point right now! You make everything about you. You never stop to listen to what I have to say, my interests..."

"Fuck your interests," I say cutting her off. "I've worked like a dog so you and Kaitlin could be comfortable. I've worshipped you. Everything you've asked for, I've given it to you. I stayed at that bullshit public defender's office instead of starting my own firm like I wanted to because you said you needed a couple more years of stable income before we took the risk. I sacrificed every day and went to a job I hated so you could work for the man you had an affair with, and now you want to say I don't listen to you!"

"You don't listen! What was the last major event I organized Ryan? Which big client fired me? Which city bid did I lose because I went in too high?"

I stare at her incredulously. I have no idea what she's talking about. What city bid? And when did a client fire her?

"See what I mean? You don't know anything about what I do all day long, but I can tell you everything about all of your cases, because I listen to you! You act like I exist to take care of Kaitlin and spread my legs on cue. When is the last time we had sex because I wanted it?"

"What the hell are you talking about? You always want it."

Janice laughs. The second the sound hits my ears I have to resist the urge to slap her. I've never even contemplated hitting a woman, but I'm standing here literally holding my arm to make sure I don't hit my wife. What the hell is happening to me?

"Ryan, I love you. I do my best to fulfill your needs. That's part of my job as your wife, but I don't always want it. Do you hear yourself? Do you think I just sit around aroused waiting for you to come and have your way with me?" She laughs again, a sound that is usually music to my ears now makes me angrier than I've ever been with my wife.

"I'm not gonna stand here and let you paint me as some arrogant misogynist," I yell much too loudly. "I'm a damn good husband!"

Janice stops laughing. Her voice turns ice cold. "Lower your voice before you wake Kaitlin! I never said you weren't a good husband. I said I need more of your attention. I need you to ask about me as a person, not your in-house booty call, not the mother of your child, not the person that takes care of your home...*ME* Ryan! I'm a person! I have needs just like you do! I'm real, with emotions... and dreams... and frustrations... and desires just like you! But your head is so far up your own ass you never even considered my needs!"

"What the hell are you talking about? I buy you everything you ask for!"

"I'm not talking about spending money!" This time it's Janice who yells. She's so angry she's practically shaking. "I'm talking about taking care of my mind, my heart, my body! For goodness sakes Ryan, the last time I tried to initiate sex, you did what you always do. You checked on Kaitlin, then sulked about *YOUR* job and completely ruined the mood. You didn't even notice the new lingerie I bought. I tried to seduce my husband and all he wanted to talk about was work!"

"Excuse the fuck out of me if my having someone's life in my hands interferes with your plans to seduce me! I don't design living rooms and order balloons for parties. Evan will go to prison if I don't do my job! While you and Asswipe sit around at lunch going over party details, I eat a sandwich at my desk while juggling cases of clients I've ever even met!"

"Get out!"

"Excuse me?"

"You heard me Ryan! Get the hell out of my house!"

"Your house? The last time I checked both of our names are on this mortgage."

"You had no trouble leaving when you thought I was screwing Clifton. What's the problem now?"

"You don't tell me to leave. I'll leave if or when I decide to go. I decide...not you," I scream as I push past her bumping her with my shoulder on my way into the guestroom.

I walk into the room and instantly remember the last time we used the room for a quickie before work. I have a visceral reaction to the room, but I'm too angry, too stubborn, and too tired to leave. I fall face first across the bed and wait for the sweet cover of darkness to overtake me. I don't have to wait very long.

Chapter 18
Michael

Kate and I sit in my office reviewing case assignments and other managerial duties when my office phone rings. My instinct is to ignore it, but I reluctantly answer.

"This is Michael."

"Hi Michael, it's Ron. I need to see you. Can you swing by my office in about an hour?"

"Ron, the last time you called me and asked me to rush over, I walked into a murder scene. I'm sure you can understand why I'm not anxious to do that again."

"Neither am I, but I do need legal advice."

"I'm not going to be working any more criminal cases. I can refer you to someone else who may be able to represent you on those matters. If you want to continue to retain Ayers & Ayers for civil matters, we'll be happy to do so."

"I don't want anyone else, Michael. I trust you. You're my attorney. I need to speak with you. This could be nothing or it could be something with major repercussions. Can you at least come over and hear me out?"

"No. You can come here and I'll listen. I'm not making any promises about representing you, but I will hear you out."

I end my call and look up to find Kate staring at me with her mouth gaping open.

"Kate, don't look at me like that. I have to hear him out. I owe him that much."

"You don't owe that murderer anything! After everything you've gone through over the past few days, I can't believe you're even allowing him to come here. Why would you put yourself in that situation? Why would you put our firm at risk like that?"

"Hold on. I'm not putting the firm at risk. Ron is a client. Let's not forget the huge retainer than comes quarterly like clockwork. I can't refuse to provide legal advice to a paying client."

"Fine. Do what you want," Kate says as she stands to leave my office. "Just don't expect me to be there the next time he puts you in a bad situation."

"I'm a big boy Kate. I took care of myself long before we got married."

Kate stops and turns to look at me. Instantly I know that last comment was over the line. Any progress I've made with my wife is now gone and in the moment, I don't care.

Ron arrives at the office about thirty minutes later. As soon as I see his face I know we're in trouble. He walks in and closes the door behind him. He jumps into conversation without preamble.

"Thirty years ago when I was a young man, I made a very stupid mistake. I've worked hard to put it behind me, but it looks like that is about to become impossible."

"What are you talking about?"

"As you know, I'm from Georgia. That's where I
planned to spend the rest of my life until I made that
impossible by being reckless." Ron wanders over to the
window and stands there staring at the city as his voice
drifts off into the distance. "I was celebrating after my
first major hostile takeover in 1986. I was at a bar down
in Macon. It was late and all of us were so drunk we
couldn't see or walk straight. There was a couple
arguing at a pool table. The guy was just as drunk as we
were. The girl was trying to leave but the guy grabbed
her by the arm. She started screaming for him to let her
go and out of nowhere he slapped her. Acting on
instinct, I rushed over and began defending the girl.
Before I knew it, my buddies joined in and the guy was
on the ground. I don't remember the exact details, but
someone had a knife. It was one of my buddies for
sure, but I had no clue which one. Whoever it was
sliced that man's face up pretty good. A couple days
later, we were all arrested and charged with attempted
murder. The guy we attacked was in critical condition
and the doctors weren't sure if he'd make it. The DA
kept threatening us with murder charges if the guy died.
He promised to drop the charges on the first person to

flip on the others. Fifteen minutes later, Jim Cochran, a man I believed to be my closest friend, lied and said I was the one with the knife. I was twenty-five years old, both of my parents were dead and I was their only child. I spent more time at Jim's house than my own. In essence, he was family. Jim turning on me meant I had no one. The other guys went along with Jim's story and accepted plea deals, leaving me as the sole defendant on the attempted murder charge. I spent a year of my life in jail awaiting trial. I spent every penny I had to find the best lawyer possible. The young man we attacked recovered and testified at my trial that the person who attacked him with the knife was wearing a long sleeve black shirt. The DA realized the error as soon as the words came out of the guy's mouth, but it was too late. My attorney attacked that point and it became the key to our defense. There were plenty of pictures of me and the guys from that night. I was wearing a long sleeve white dress shirt with my sleeves rolled up to my elbows. Guess who was wearing the black long sleeve shirt?"

"Jim?" I reply quizzically.

"You got it. My only friend in the world who was more like a brother to me, lied and blamed me for his crime. I was acquitted, but everyone in Macon still believed I was guilty. I had no one to turn to. My business folded while I was in jail awaiting trial, and I only had $300 in the bank."

"What did you do?"

"I took that $300 and relocated to Charlotte. I got a job at an investment firm and as soon as I could afford it, I legally changed my name from Carroll Ronald Hunt to Ron Edahl and started my life over. I met Patty a couple years later and told her everything. She's the only one I ever told...until now."

"Why now? Why are you telling me this?"

"Because the man we attacked that night was Sean Tenney."

"Are you shitting me? U.S. Senator Sean Tenney?"

"The one and only."

"You and your drunk asshole friends beat the shit out of a Senator?"

"He wasn't a Senator back then. He was a drunk kid who slapped his date. I stepped in to defend her!"

"You can try to tell that story, but it's not going to fly seeing as how you just avoided prison time using the exact same defense!"

"It's the truth!"

I hang my head. This thing with Ron just grew arms and legs and walked up and slapped both of us. How the hell am I supposed to spin this one? A one-time accident is one thing, but now Ron has a history of losing his temper and becoming violent against black men. Another thought occurs to me.

"Ron please tell me the woman Tenney was with was black."

"No, she was white, and I know how it sounds, but Michael you know me. I'm not a racist."

"I know that, but Sean Tenney is the biggest race baiter since Al Sharpton and you just avoided prison time after beating a black teenager to death. If he gets wind of this, it's going to be very ugly. The city is still recovering after the riots surrounding the Keith

Lamont Scott shooting. We can't handle another scandal right now."

"It's too late. He already knows and he's on his way to Charlotte right now to lead a march against me."

Chapter 19
Ryan

After last night's fight with Janice, and the very
uncomfortable staff meeting this morning, I'm relieved
to finally be able to focus on work. Kate and I sit in her
office pouring over documents for Evan's case. We
have exactly one week until jury selection begins and
I'm scared shitless for Evan. Bart is determined to see
Evan behind bars and the case is gaining momentum in
the media. I think we should request a change of venue,
but Kate believes it will be pointless. When it comes to
the death of a child, there won't be a jury pool in the
state that won't be tainted. She believes we have a
greater chance of getting a jury here where the citizens
are more educated and polished than some of the more
rural areas. When we begin to present the medical

evidence, it will be important to have jurors that will be able to understand and follow the evidence.

Out of the corner of my eye I see Kate's hand rush to her belly. I'm at her side in an instant.

"Kate, are you okay?"

"I'm sure it's okay. I've been having sharp pains on and off for a couple days now."

"Have you been to the doctor?"

Kate chuckles. "No. It's my first pregnancy. I don't want to be seen as one of those women that overacts over every discomfort."

"Does Michael know?"

"No, and you're not going to tell him...Aaaaah!"

Kate doubles over and instantly I know something is wrong. I dash from the office as fast as I can. I rush past Michael's secretary who's busy typing at warp speed and doesn't put forth any effort to stop me from rushing into his office.

"Michael! It's Kate. There's something wrong!"

A look of terror flashes on Michael's face as he jumps from his seat. He's rushing past me in a second leaving his client Ron Edahl looking equally as frightened. I follow Michael back to Kate's office. I see the blood before I hear the screams. Other associates are now rushing to see what's going. I yell for someone to call 911, but Michael's voice cuts me off.

"We don't have time." He scoops Kate up into his arms and yells as he runs towards me. "Come on! We have to get her to the hospital now!"

A benefit of working in the South Park area, is the ease at which we can get to Carolina Medical Center without running into downtown traffic. During the drive, I break nearly every traffic law as Michael pleads with Kate to hang in there. I want to ask questions, but I know better than to speak. I drive at break neck speed until we pull into the emergency room bay. Within seconds Michael has Kate inside the hospital, demanding a room for her. I catch only a glimpse of Kate's pale face as Michael whisks her to the back with the nurses close on his heels. I park the car and sit for a moment willing myself not to look at the backseat. I already know it's stained with Kate's blood. My mind travels a few moments back to the sound of Michael's voice as he comforted his wife. A sharp pain shoots through my heart and I realize I don't want to wait to hear the news about Kate alone. I want the only person that knows how to comfort me. I pull my phone from my pocket and dial the number from memory.

"Hello."

I pause for a second as emotions run through me at the sound of her voice. I feel myself begin to cry.

"Ryan? What's wrong? Where are you?"

"CMC," I squeak out through my tears.

"Why? What's wrong? Are you hurt?" Janice practically shouts as terror creeps into her voice.

"It's not me. It's Kate. There's so much blood."

"I'm on my way."

I allow the phone to drop from my hands as the grief runs through me. The truth is I don't know if I'm crying for Kate and Michael or Janice and me. It's been such a rough few weeks. As mad as Janice's words made me last night, now that I'm sober I know she was

right. I can't remember ever asking her about her job.
It's always about me and whatever client I'm defending.
Janice has been there since undergrad pushing me to
succeed and reach for my dreams. She put her life on
hold when we found out we were expecting Kaitlin. We
had no plans of having children. I can still remember
Janice warning me her birth control was weakened by
the antibiotics she'd taken. She'd developed an inner
ear infection while fighting a really bad cold that took a
while to clear up. The doctor advised her to use backup
birth control for a few weeks. She tried to get me to go
out and buy a box of condoms, but as usual, I didn't
listen. I told her married couples didn't need condoms.
If we became pregnant then it was clearly time for us to
become parents. Janice didn't agree with me, but she
didn't fight me on it. Five weeks later, we learned
Kaitlin was on the way and Janice spent the next couple
of months puking up everything she ate. She was too
weak to work and had to quit her job. My tears turn
into embarrassing sobbing as I realize that even when
my wife was sick from carrying our child, I didn't care
for her as I should have. Her mother did the bulk of
the work. Janice gave up her career until Kaitlin was a

year old and I never once said thank you. I repaid her by acting like a complete ass the first time she showed me she wasn't perfect.

I don't know how long I sat there crying my sorrows onto my shirt before Janice arrived. Once I saw her an overwhelming feeling of gratitude flowed through me.

"I'm sorry Janice. I've been a complete ass. I don't know how you've put up with me this long, but if you'll give me a chance to change I promise I'll do my best to be a better husband."

Janice, clearly taken aback by my words begins to tear up. "Ryan, this is music to my ears, but where is it coming from?"

"I just watched Michael nearly lose his wife and it reminded me how close I am to losing my own."

"What are you talking about? What happened to Kate?"

"I don't know. One minute we were working, the next she was doubled over in pain and there was blood, so much blood." I nod towards the back seat as I say the last sentence.

Janice turns and notices the blood in the back seat for the first time. Her hand instantly flies to her mouth. "Oh my God! What about the baby?"

"I don't know. I haven't been able to get out of the car."

"Come on Ryan. We have to get inside."

"I can't Janice. Not like this..."

Janice leans over and places her hands on my face. It's the first time she's touched me in weeks and it feels like balm for my wounded soul. She gently lifts my face until our eyes meet. "Ryan, Kate offered to help you when no one else would. At the very least she deserves to know you're here to support her. You and I were good the moment you said you've been an ass. Now wipe your face and let's get inside and let Michael and Kate know we're here for them."

I smile slightly. Janice is my backbone. She motivates me better than anyone I've ever known. It dawns on me Janice doesn't know I'm now working for Ayers & Ayers. "Janice, I didn't get to tell you with all we've been going through, but you should know I work for Kate and Michael now."

"What? Since when?"

"Since Thomas fired me?"

"What!? Why did he fire you?"

"Because he's an asshole who couldn't handle me getting the help I needed without him."

Janice drops her head. "There goes our plan to relocate and start over in a small town."

"Maybe we still can," I say not bothering to hold my smile inside. "I make more money now. We might be able to leave sooner than we thought."

"I quit my job Ryan. We'll be pinching pennies even with your raise."

"You didn't ask me how big the raise is," I say with a smile before exiting the car. I don't know what we are about to walk into, but I'm happy we're walking into it together. It feels weird to be happy before going to find out if my bosses have lost their child, but I am. No matter what news we face, knowing we're facing it together makes it much more bearable. I'm sure Michael and Kate will appreciate the support.

Chapter 20
Michael

I don't know how long I've been sitting here waiting for an update on Kate and our baby, but the sight of the doctor makes me feel like I'm experiencing air for the first time.

"Mr. Ayers..."

I leap to my feet and cut him off. "Is my wife okay?"

"It appears Kate suffered a placental abruption. She is stable, but the condition is very serious. The placenta has separated slightly from Kate's uterus."

"What about my son?"

"The baby is stable for now, but we have to keep Kate here until she delivers."

"What? She's only 28 weeks. You're gonna keep her for 12 weeks?"

"Mr. Ayers, Kate won't be able to carry to term. Placental abruptions can be fatal to both mom and baby, so our goal is to allow Kate to continue with the pregnancy as long as it is safe for her to do so. We want to give the baby the best chance at survival so we are administering meds to help his lungs develop. We're giving Kate one unit of blood to replace what she's lost. We're going to monitor both mom and baby very closely and if there is any sign that her condition is worsening we'll deliver the baby at once."

"How did this happen? She was fine one minute and the next we were on our way here."

"The exact cause is not known. In most cases, there is some sort of trauma, but in a small number of cases, like Kate's, the placenta separates for reasons we can't determine until after delivery and even then, there's a chance we may not be able to determine a definite diagnosis. What's important is that you got Kate here quickly and she's being monitored closely."

"Can I see her?"

"Yes, but please allow her to rest. It's important that she sleeps as much as possible. Her body is experiencing a very serious trauma."

"I just need to see her," I say as my eyes start to fill with tears.

"Michael."

I turn at the sound of my name. A woman I've never seen before is walking towards me with a man walking slightly behind her. It takes a moment before I recognize the man is Ryan. I quickly remember everyone at the office is probably worried sick about Kate.

"Doc can you give me a second? I forgot I need to send instructions back to the office."

"Sure Mr. Ayers. Just have one of the nurses direct you to Kate's room when you're ready."

I extend my hand to the doctor. He quickly accepts and offers me a firm shake. "I can't thank you enough for saving my..." I say before the tears try to return effectively causing my throat to close. The doctor uses his free arm to grip my shoulder and give it a supportive squeeze.

"No thanks necessary," he replies before releasing me and turning to leave.

I take a moment to gather myself before turning back around to face Ryan and the woman. When I turn around again I notice the woman is leaning into Ryan. My eyes travel to their hands which are intertwined and I assume this woman is his wife.

"Michael, is Kate going to be okay?" Ryan speaks up snapping my attention back to his face.

"Kate and the baby are both stable but they are going to have to stay here until after the baby is born. There's been a serious complication that's going to require around the clock monitoring."

"I'm sorry to hear that. Is there anything we can do?" The woman speaks up prompting me to really get a good look at her face. She's beautiful. Not in the traditional sweet girl next door look sense that Kate possesses, but in a sultry way. She seems to be beyond Ryan's league, but I think many would say the same about Kate and me.

"Michael this is my wife Janice. She rushed over as soon as I told her Kate was here. She hasn't met Kate yet, but I speak of the two of you often so she wanted to show her support as well."

I extend my hand. "Thank you Janice. We appreciate you being here. Have you two been here the whole time?"

"Yes, but we stayed over there trying not to invade your private moment."

I chuckle slightly surprising myself. "I could have used the interruption. I think I held my breath until the doctor told me they're both going to be okay."

"Ryan has been the same way," she says as she glances over at her husband. The way she looks at him reminds me of the way Kate looks at me during the good times.

"Thank you Ryan. If you hadn't sprang into action..."

"Don't mention it," Ryan says cutting me off. "I did what anyone would have done. Look, we know you're anxious to get to your wife and baby so we won't hold you. We just wanted you to know we're here if you need anything.

"I appreciate that. There are a few things you could take care of for me if you don't mind."

"Sure. Say the word."

***

I walk into Kate's room and instantly my stomach jumps into my throat. Seeing my tiny wife laying there with tubes running everywhere and monitors beeping in cadence, reminds me of the final few months of my father's life. It was in those months that I learned who my father really was. The gulf that separated us slowly closed until I became like an extension of him, spending hours at his side working quietly as he slept. I can't bear the idea of going through the same thing with Kate. My father was relatively young to die, but he had an opportunity to live and experience life. Kate is young and just beginning to live. We have plans to travel the world and experience each continent together. We've talked about growing old and watching our grandchildren grow up. Without Kate, nothing in life will matter. She is the best of me.

An errant tear escapes my eye as I stand with my feet cemented to the space just inside of the door. I want to move. I want to rush to her and take her in my arms, but my body literally disobeys my mental commands. More tears are now flowing and I hear ragged breathing. It takes a moment for me to realize the breathing is my own. I try to tell myself to be strong for Kate, to locate my testicles and force them to drop back down, but nothing is happening. I begin to feel dizzy and the room starts to spin. I know I'm experiencing another panic attack, but I can't stop it. I feel my hand rush to my throat to loosen my tie. The sound of gasping for air replaces the ragged breathing and I feel my face growing hot. I struggle to gain control of my breathing, but my efforts are futile. The room begins going dark around the corners and I find myself welcoming the darkness.

"Michael."

I hear Kate calling me from the darkness and I begin to pray for it to overtake me so I can join her.

"Michael," she calls again. "Michael, breathe. Breathe Honey. I'm okay. I promise, I'm okay. Just breathe. There you go....yes....in and out. Slow down. Enjoy the air as it fills your lungs. Everything is okay. The baby and I are both going to be fine."

It takes a moment for me to come to myself, but when I do I immediately rush over to Kate. How is it possible that she is the one in the hospital bed, yet she's comforting me?

"I should be the one calming you down," I say trying to hide my embarrassment.

"I was fine the moment the doctor told me our baby is okay."

"But how are you? Are you in any pain?"

"No Mike. I'm okay. I promise."

"How long were you in pain before you said anything?"

"I had a little discomfort, but I wasn't in any real pain until it all hit me at once. I didn't really have a chance to catch my breath or process what was happening. One minute I was talking to Ryan..." Kate's voice catches in her throat as realization sets in. "Oh my goodness I must have scared everyone half to death. Do they know I'm okay?"

"Shhhh. Don't worry. Ryan is on his way back to the office to let everyone know you and the baby are going to be okay."

"He stayed here with you all this time?"

"Well, he didn't exactly stay with me. I didn't even know he was here until he and his wife approached me as I was heading back here to see you."

"Janice was here too?"

"You know his wife? He said the two of you have never met."

"I haven't formally met her, but Ryan talks about her nonstop. I'm happy she was here for him. That means things are back on track with them."

"What does that mean?"

"Nothing, don't worry about it. What about work? If I'm stuck here in the hospital, I can work on briefs and such to help keep the cases on track while I'm out."

I smile at my wife. She's in the hospital and still thinking of everyone except herself.

"Why are you smiling at me like that?"

"Because even after all you've been through, you're still concerned about everyone else. It's sweet, but I'm not letting you work."

"Michael we have a full case load and Evan's trial begins in a week. I can't leave him hanging."

"Ryan will handle Evan's case."

"He's not prepared to go up against Bart alone."

"Then he needs to get prepared. Why are we paying a litigator who can't litigate?"

"He can litigate, he just doesn't have any experience with murder cases. He needs someone to walk him through it. He'll be a great second chair, but he's not ready to do this alone."

"He's gotta cut his teeth sometime Kate. We don't have the manpower to coddle him any longer. Now this isn't up for discussion. No more talk about work. Making sure you and our son are safe is my first priority. The doctor said you need to rest. Talking about work won't help you rest."

Kate sighs and I know she's not happy with me, but she surprises me by relenting. She closes her eyes and takes a deep breath. Tears start to slowly pour down her face. "Michael, what if my body can't hold on to our baby?"

"Hey," I whisper. "Don't talk like that. Listen to that heartbeat," I urge. "Our little guy is a champ and you are completely equipped to be his mommy. You will hold onto him until it's safe for him to come out."

Kate looks up at me and for the first time in a long time I see fear. I realize that like me, Kate likes to focus on work so she doesn't have to think about her problems. I don't know how I've missed this about my wife, but it's clear to me she wants to think about anything except the risk of losing our baby.

I quickly remove my shoes, blood stained pants, and jacket. Kate knows what's coming and I see the worry start to leave her face. I slip in bed behind my wife and pull her into my arms. Without a word she snuggles into me and I begin to stroke her hair. I'm not a perfect man, but here in this moment, I can be the comfort and security my wife needs. Neither of us knows what tomorrow will hold, but we slip into a peaceful slumber knowing that for right now, all is okay.

Chapter 21
Ryan

A week has passed since Kate was rushed to the hospital and it's been pure chaos every day in the office. Michael has stopped by every morning, but between Kate and the trouble his client Ron Edahl has dragged him into, he hasn't been able to provide me with any support for Evan's case. That's why I'm meeting with H.E. Higgins this morning. Without Kate's help, I need the private investigator to help me uncover loopholes in the prosecution's case.

Mr. Higgins' office is quiet and I find myself wondering how he maintains such a large suite of offices alone. There is a large receptionist desk, but it's completely bare so it doesn't look as though he employs a receptionist. The walls are adorned with beautiful pictures of the city of Charlotte. I'm standing and slowly walking from picture to picture when a short bald man walks from the back of the building to greet me.

"You must be Ryan," Higgins says with a deep Carolinian twang I wasn't expecting to come from a black man.

"And you're Mr. Higgins?"

"Just Higgins will do. What can I do for you?"

"Kate told me she spoke to you about helping us on the Evan Reynolds case, but since she's been hospitalized I haven't been able to find out how much information she's given you."

"She hasn't given me much to go on. Fill me in."

I spend the next thirty minutes giving Higgins everything I know about Evan, Lisa, and the day their baby girl drowned. I tell him about Bart and his determination to see Evan convicted. I hold back Kate's insinuation that Lisa Reynolds could be a suspect. I'm not one hundred percent sure why I keep the information to myself. Maybe there's something inside of me that won't let me throw a grieving mother under the bus...even if it would save my client. I won't be able to live with myself if I keep one innocent person out of prison by putting another innocent person in his place.

The drive from Higgins' office to the courthouse was a short one, but my mind was racing the entire time. I drive in a complete blur, unable to focus on anything except the start of Evan's trial. I walk into the courthouse and stand in the security line for courthouse workers. Ever since the former chief of police went rogue and shot up a courtroom, we've all had to go through extra layers of security. I empty my pockets, placing my belongings in the bin on the table when a voice behind me makes the hairs on the back of my neck stand up.

"Well look who is....it's the baby killer's lawyer."

I don't bother turning around to address Bart's childish banter. I'm nervous enough as it is handling the case alone. The last thing I need is to let Bart get inside of my head and ruin my focus.

"Oh, no don't be like that," Bart says with mock tenderness. "Just because we're on opposite sides of this thing, that doesn't mean we can't be friends."

I walk through the metal detector without incident and wait for the deputy to pass me my belongings. I keep my expression blank and my eyes trained straight ahead. I cringe when Bart slaps me on the back and leans in to whisper in my ear.

"Listen, I meant what I said. You and I aren't enemies. You seem like a standup guy. Why don't we grab a beer after court today?"

I finally speak. "Are you serious? Why would I want to drink with you?"

"You can't take these cases so seriously. I know it's your first murder case, but you've been around long enough to know how this works. When a defense attorney and a prosecutor have an amicable relationship, everyone wins."

I back away and look Bart in the eyes. I can't believe he's serious. "Bart, if you wanted an amicable relationship you shouldn't have pressed charges against an innocent man. I'm not keeping my distance from you because you're a prosecutor, I'm staying away because you're the worst kind of prosecutor. You don't care about these clients. You don't even really care about the law. You're trying to make a name for yourself. What are you working up to? Judge? Newsflash asshole, no one will vote for a man that railroads the poor to boost his conviction rate."

I grab the rest of my belongings and walk away from Bart feeling confident. Despite what he and Thomas both think, I'm going to put up one hell of a defense for Evan, starting with my very first motion. The courtroom is full and I find myself becoming nauseas as soon as I enter. I spot a few familiar faces in the gallery and decide to do something I've never been brave enough to do. I walk over to the reporter from Action 9 News and introduce myself.

"Hi Ms. Warren, my name is Ryan Du Bois and I..."

"I know exactly who you are," the blonde reporter says with a smile as she stands and extends her hand.

We shake as I quickly try to say what I need to say before Bart enters the courtroom. "If you'd be interested in sitting down with me, I have some information that might be very useful to you," I say with a smile.

"Well, I am a reporter and you do work for one of the most talked about firms in Charlotte. When can we chat?"

"Later this evening if you're free. How about you give me one of your cards and I'll call you with the specifics?"

I'm relieved when she reaches into her pocket and pulls out a business card without asking for mine in return. I still haven't received mine from Ayers & Ayers so it was nice not to be asked for one. I grab the card from her and nod as I walk quickly to the front of the room. I snag my position at the defense table just as Bart enters the room. There is a subtle buzz that builds as he walks towards the prosecution table, but I try not to let it bother me. It's no secret who the star of today's show is, but I'm confident I can hold my own.

Bart and I both begin to unload our briefcases as we begin the inevitable wait for the judge to join us. I don't understand why judges take so long to assume the bench. There are a select few, and by few I mean one or two that are meticulous about starting on time. Everyone else just meanders around and takes their sweet time while the rest of us grow old waiting. When the door opens, veteran Judge Alex Holder walks in, everyone stands as he takes his place behind the bench.

Judge Holder has been a Superior Court Judge for the better part of the last twenty years. His rulings have been fair, but his sentencing tends to lean on the lighter side. Rumor has it he has been heard complaining about the overcrowding of American prisons and the burden it places on tax payers. Of course, this is courthouse gossip, which means it may have a glimmer of truth, but it's still about as reliable as a supermarket tabloid. In this instance, for Evan's sake, I am praying the gossip is right.

After the usual preamble, Evan is led into the courtroom wearing the suit I provided for him. His bruises have healed and despite his current residence at the county jail, he looks fresh and well rested. This is a point I have hammered into him over the past few weeks. Although Evan insists he has no desire to go on living after losing his daughter, I remain committed to my decision to help him stay out of prison. I have convinced myself that years from now, once Evan has properly grieved, he will thank me for helping him when he didn't have the strength, energy, or will to help himself. It sounds like a fantasy, but the reality is, I simply would not be able to live with myself if I didn't do the right thing. As disturbed as I may be about Evan's daughter drowning on his watch, something about this case just hasn't added up since the very beginning. I've been distracted by my own personal issues, and now the issues at work, but from this moment until the jury renders their verdict, my focus will be Evan Reynolds.

"Your Honor, before we begin, I'd like to make a motion to have my client's post arrest interview suppressed."

"Objection Your Honor! Mr. Reynolds voluntarily gave a statement to the officers. He was read his rights and waived his right to an attorney. Defense has no grounds for this motion," Bart says as he leaps to his feet. If this immediate objection is any indication of

Bart's preparedness, my attempt to ambush him was futile.

"Actually Your Honor, not long after the arrest, it was discovered that my client suffered from a debilitating tumor that significantly impaired his memory and caused significant pain that left him unable to properly weigh the magnitude of his decisions."

"This tumor is the crux of Mr. Reynold's defense. Mr. Du Bois can at least wait until we have a jury selected before he starts laying out his case," Bart says through gritted teeth.

"I'm not laying out our case, but Your Honor, the medical evidence surrounding tumors of this type are clear. I do have an expert prepared to testify that the tumor severely hampered Evan Reynolds' mental capacity."

"Mr. Du Bois is forgetting that Evan Reynolds worked for months with this tumor. Not once was he written up at work for errors or incidents involving competence. In fact, the State has interviewed former co-workers who will testify that they had no indication whatsoever that Evan suffered from any type of medical condition. No changes were seen in his behavior or performance."

"My client should not be penalized for doing his job well under extreme circumstances. His co-workers are not doctors. They can't testify to effects of the tumor on Mr. Reynolds' brain."

"On that point I can't disagree," Judge Holder interjects silencing Bart and me. "You can challenge their testimony during cross examination. Your motion to suppress the post arrest interview is denied."

Bart looks over at me with a smug expression and it takes every ounce of restraint I have not to leap over and throttle him.

Chapter 22
Michael

Sitting down with Brigida Mack is not how I want to spend my Friday afternoon. I'd much rather be sitting at my wife's side at the hospital. However, Ron's past has caught up with him and the negative attention he's receiving must be cauterized to stop the bleeding to his business and personal life as soon as possible. Sean Tenney and the local NAACP representatives have organized marches all week long. They've been on every local news channel and after last night's CNN broadcast, the story has gone national. So far, everything has been peaceful, but last night Ron received a death threat. He and Patty have moved to an undisclosed location, but remaining silent is no longer an option. Ron has to speak publicly and tell his side of the story. So far, all anyone has heard is how Tenney was attacked. It's time to change the conversation.

"I want to thank you both for sitting down with me," Brigida says with a warm smile.

"Thank you for this opportunity," Ron says with a sadness in his tone and eyes that would reduce even the strongest man to tears.

"Yes, thank you so much Brigida. We appreciate you making room in your schedule to sit down with us. It's important Ron be able to tell his side of the story and dispel the accusations being made against him."

"It really is my pleasure," Brigida says with another smile that appears more forced than the last.

For a moment I think about canceling the interview and running for the hills. Something feels off, but I ignore the feeling and look directly into the camera as the producer begins to count down.

"Welcome to a special edition of *Evenings with Brigida*. This evening we're sitting down with local businessman Ron Edahl and his attorney Michael Ayers. For our viewers who aren't familiar with Ron, I want to fill you guys in before we begin. Ron Edahl has been a member of the Charlotte community for roughly thirty years. During this time, he has contributed to countless charities and held positions on many boards of nonprofit organizations throughout the state of North Carolina. On the morning of June 21st, Ron and his wife Patty were awakened by the screams of their daughter. Reacting like any parent would, Ron ran to the defense of his daughter. Ron, why don't you tell our viewers what happened next?"

I squirm uncomfortably in my seat. This is not the line of questioning we agreed to. Ron is supposed to be talking about what happened thirty years ago. I know I have to speak up before Ron says something to make the situation worse.

"Actually Brigida, Ron is still grieving over his daughter. He's not at a place to speak of her publicly just yet. We're here to talk about the recent accusations that have been made against my client."

Brigida, ever the professional, quickly pivots and continues speaking as though this is all a part of our plan. "Mr. Edahl, Sean Tenney, Democratic U.S.

Senator from Georgia is here in Charlotte along with members of the NAACP and protestors from the Black Lives Matter movement to protest your recent suspended sentence. Protests have been going on all week and are expected to continue throughout the weekend. They are calling for a reversal of Judge Lewis' decision and making some very serious allegations against you. Would you care to comment on those?"

"Brigida, the first thing I want everyone to know is that I am not now, nor have I ever been a racist. Over thirty years ago, I went out to celebrate my first major business deal. While there, my friends and I witnessed a man strike his date. We reacted to protect the young woman. During the altercation, the young man suffered cuts to his face. I did not know then, nor do I know with absolute certainty now, who cut the man's face. What I do in fact know, is that I did not cut anyone. As it often happens in cases with multiple defendants, the prosecutor offered a deal to the first person to agree to testify against the rest of the group. As it turned out, I was the only person who did not accept the prosecutor's deal. I did not have the information the prosecutor needed and I refused to lie on the stand.

When the man who was injured that night recovered, he testified that the person who cut his face was wearing a black shirt. Evidence from that night proved I was wearing a white shirt. I was acquitted and have worked very hard to put that terrible experience behind me. Unfortunately, all these years later Sean Tenney, the man who was cut, the person who testified to what his attacker was wearing, is now claiming I was the one responsible for the cuts to his face."

"And you maintain that your actions that night were not racially motivated?"

"I jumped into action when I saw a man strike a woman. Race had nothing to do with it."

"As I'm sure you know, Senator Tenney tells a very different story about that night."

"I do know that, but the fact remains, I was acquitted. Senator Tenney's own testimony during the trial excludes me as the attacker with the knife. The prosecutor presented pictures of my friends and I during the trial. Only one person in the photo wore all black and that person wasn't me."

"The protestors here in Charlotte are convinced you have been able to escape prison time because of your wealth and influence."

"That's nonsense," I jump in. "Ron went to trial and was found not guilty. He's spent his life, not as an angry man who was railroaded by a misguided prosecutor, but as a man willing to roll up his sleeves and work to help his community. But instead of allowing Ron to grieve the loss of his daughter in private, Sean Tenney has brought this unwanted attention to Ron and the city of Charlotte. Many of the protestors are not even residents of the state. I don't mean any disrespect to Senator Tenney, but his efforts are only driving a deeper wedge into an already divided city."

"How do you explain your client's ability to attack two African American men decades apart, and escape prison both times?"

I narrow my eyes at Brigida. She's supposed to be the fairest on air personality in the city. If she's coming at us this hard, Ron has a long uphill battle before him. "My client did not *escape* jail time. Thirty years ago a prosecutor dangled a deal in front of a group of young men to force them to turn on each other. There's a reason tactics like that are frowned upon today. It basically encourages assailants to lie so they can save themselves. It backfired due to the prosecution's own evidence that exonerated my client. Ron lost everything while sitting in jail for over a year waiting for his trial, without so much as an apology after the prosecutor's dirty tricks were revealed. That experience changed my client, so he relocated here to Charlotte and worked hard to start his life over. He hasn't even had a speeding ticket since that night. I want every father out there to imagine he was awakened by the screams of his daughter. Imagine you act on impulse and rush to save your baby girl, but find a man on top of her in her bedroom. I don't know a single father in the world that wouldn't react in the same way Ron reacted. We are deeply saddened by the death of Khalil Jeffries and we offer our sympathy to his family, but members of the community along with Senator Tenney are trying to turn this into something that it's not. Everyone is forgetting that my client is also grieving. He also lost his only child that morning. Race had nothing to do with what happened. Furthermore, it's irresponsible for those who are supposed to be community leaders to come to Charlotte and spread lies and misinformation. Their presence here is only pouring salt into the wounds of our city."

"So you're saying it's a coincidence that both of the men your client attacked were black?"

"I'm saying my client did not attack anyone. In both instances, he stood up to defend young women who he believed to be in trouble. It would have mattered if the aggressor were a green-eyed Martian. Ron did what any man with an ounce of respect for women would do. He's an upstanding member of this community with a company that holds more minorities on its Board of Directors than any other company in the southeast. He most certainly is not a racist."

Brigida offers another one of her fake smiles and I know she's about to bury us. I silently pray as the words fall from her well painted lips, but as soon as I hear them I know my prayer was futile. Appearing on this show was a very bad idea.

"I know I speak for the African American community of Charlotte," Brigida begins still wearing the same fake smile, "when I say being willing to employ African Americans means nothing if you attack black men for being with white women."

Chapter 23
Ryan

Sitting across the table having drinks with a beautiful woman who is not my wife is foreign to me. Something about Jocelyn Warren makes this encounter feel much more intimate than it should. Even worse, I can feel myself becoming aroused. I quickly speed the conversation along. I don't need to stay in the presence of this woman a second longer than absolutely necessary.

"Ms. Warren, what I'm saying is that Evan Reynolds is a proud father. He loves all of his children. There is no way he could have intentionally hurt his daughter. There's no reason for the D.A. to be charging him with murder. Even involuntary manslaughter is a stretch."

"But a child is dead. If what you are telling me is true, I feel sorry for your client, but his daughter drowned on his watch. Are we supposed to ignore that?"

"What if I told you that the only reason Bart Winslow is so set on getting Evan convicted of murder is because he's trying to re-build his reputation so he can run for judge next term?"

"Is that true?" Jocelyn has more concern on her face than I expected, but I don't back down.

"I have it on very good authority that for the past year, Bart has been trying to overcome the Shamika Carrington debacle and keep his name fresh in voters' minds."

"Are you willing to let me quote you on this?"

"Absolutely not. Like I said over the phone, everything we discuss has to be off the record."

"The story does me no good without a credible source. With the President of the United States labeling everything as fake news, the media is under intense scrutiny."

"I respect your position. Don't take my word for it. Do some discrete digging on your own and you'll see that I'm right."

I watch Jocelyn's delicate features as the wheels of creativity in her brain begin to turn. I can see the story she is piecing together and it takes everything in me not to smile. She may never admit it, but she's just been hooked and I have her right where I want her. With only the smallest hint of credibility, she's going to run the story. She's right about the present climate of the media. They are under a microscope. The rush to be the first to break a story is a double-edged sword, one that most journalists fall on daily. As long as it sells papers, or drives traffic to a website, stories are printed that contain only a fraction of truth. If Jocelyn runs this story on Bart, there may be hope in swaying the public over to Evan's side. Regardless of what anyone says, unless a jury is sequestered, there is always a chance they will watch the news, read the paper, or log onto social media. Once a person reads, sees, or hears something, the bell can't be un-rung. The judge will give the jury their instructions as to what can be considered when trying to reach a verdict. The jurors may do their best to follow those rules, but somewhere on a subconscious level, things they've heard outside of the courtroom, pillow talk with their spouse, things said on the stand that were stricken from the record...those things will always be lurking in the back of the juror's mind. The mind never forgets. It's the ultimate storage facility. Memories, thoughts, fears, and ideas we don't want to remember are always lurking in the shadows waiting to haunt us at the most inconvenient times. Try as we may, we can't control when our mind throws those things back into play.

"At least give me a hint. Who in Bart's circle is most likely to let something slip?"

I smile at Jocelyn. This is the question I've been waiting for. "Remember Judge Roberts?"

"The Judge that just retired? Of course. We ran a piece about his retirement a few weeks ago."

"Did you know he has a fondness for the bottle?"

"Everyone knows about the rumors, but I just assumed that's all they were."

"No. It's fact. Judge Roberts has been drinking too much for years, but it never really affected his performance behind the bench. Even drunk, the man controlled his courtroom without incident. Now that's he's retired, he's a little less discrete with his drinking. His favorite watering hole is over off of Rea Road and Ballantyne Commons Parkway. It's called *The Wet Whistle Bar and Lounge.* If you can catch him over there you can get two stories at once."

I watch as Jocelyn thinks this over. A thought occurs to her as her face becomes inquisitive. "Why me Ryan? There were at least a dozen reporters in that courtroom. Why did you walk over to me?"

I've asked myself the same question repeatedly. On the surface, I want to say it was because she was the closest to me when I walked in the courtroom, or because she caught my attention first, but I know both are lies. I've had a small crush on Jocelyn for years. Every time I see her, I'm taken by how beautiful she is. If I'm completely honest with myself, I'm still hurt by Janice's admission of having feelings for Clifton. Maybe walking up to Jocelyn was my juvenile way of getting back at Janice. I know I won't say or do anything inappropriate, but sitting here with this beautiful woman is doing wonders for my wounded ego. I know better to admit any of this to Jocelyn or anyone else.

"I walked over to the first reporter I saw. I was rushing to speak to someone before Bart walked in and saw me."

"So you and I sitting here enjoying drinks is a purely professional coincidence?"

Without realizing it's coming, I blush. I try to recover quickly, but it's too late. Jocelyn sees it and I know I'm in trouble.

***

Walking back into the courtroom, I am more poised following my meeting with Jocelyn the previous night. It may take her a few days, but Jocelyn is known for covering the stories all the other journalists shy away from. I know she will print exactly what I need to sway the public's opinion of Evan. I take a seat at the defense table feeling confident about the start of the trial today. After yesterday's jury selection, which did not go my way, I know I have my work cut out for me.

I glance at my watch as Bart waltzes into the courtroom wearing his arrogance about as well as he wears his expensive suits. I wonder for a moment if anything he owns isn't tailored. For all of the rumors surrounding his hate of his father, I can't help but wonder if he's living off of his father's wealth. There's no way a state employee can afford the clothes Bart wears, even without having a family to support. Without bothering to glance in my direction, Bart takes his seat and begins readying himself for the proceedings. I note how he spares me the normal taunting expression and brush it off as a blessing. I don't know if I'll be able to hold my secret inside if he tries to bait me today. I want so badly to take him down a peg.

The side door to the courtroom opens and instead of the judge coming in, his clerk walks over towards my table.

"Judge Holder needs to see you in chambers immediately."

She does not give me a chance to ask questions before walking over to Bart and telling him the same thing.

Bart and I both grab our things and follow the mousey clerk back to Judge Holder's chambers. Right away I notice the Sherriff as well as two deputies are already waiting along with the judge. As soon as the door closes behind us, Judge Holder jumps right into conversation.

"Evan Reynolds was found hanging in his cell this morning."

"What! How the hell could he have hung himself?"

"Watch your tone Mr. Du Bois," Judge Holder admonishes. "I know you're upset to learn about your client, but you still need to watch your decorum in my chambers."

"Is he dead?"

I stare at Bart incredulously. How can he be so callous when we're talking about someone's life?

"Yes," the judge replies. "It appears he hung himself sometime overnight. The body was already cold when he was found this morning."

"Why am I just being notified? And what did he use to hang himself? Aren't reasonable safety precautions taken for all inmates?"

"Yes, but as you know, when one wants to take their own life, a way is usually found," the Sherriff speaks for the first time.

"This just saved the tax payers thousands of dollars," Bart interjects. "A baby killer is off the streets and we didn't have to waste time and money on a trial."

I lunge at Bart before I even realize what's happening. It takes the Sherriff plus both of the deputies to pull me off of him. I don't succeed in doing harm, but it wasn't for lack of trying. I don't think I've ever genuinely hated anyone the way I hate Bart Winslow right now. He's intentionally provocative and goes out of his way to hurt people.

"You're a sick son of bitch and I can't wait to expose you for the piece of shit you really are," I yell completely forgetting where we are. Though I'm still being held back by the deputies, I try to lunge for him again. Fortunately for him, the deputies have death grips on both of my arms.

Bart laughs. "If you think Jocelyn is going to help you with that, you're sadly mistaken," Bart says as he winks at me.

I stop squirming at his last remark. I watch as Bart leaves the judge's chambers without another word. The only way Bart could have known about my meeting with Jocelyn was if she told him. Is that how he has been able to keep negative stories about his improper prosecution of the poor out of the papers? Is he sleeping with one of the most influential reporters in the city?

"Mr. Du Bois," Judge Holder says bringing my attention back to him. "We realize how upset you are, so we are going to forgive your outburst, but make no mistake, if anything like this ever happens in my chambers again you will be held in contempt. Are we clear?"

"Yes Your Honor," I say sheepishly as the deputies release me and I sink back down into my chair. The weight of learning of Evan's death feels like it's pulling my soul closer and closer to the pit of despair. "Has anyone notified his next of kin?" I ask the Sherriff knowing Lisa Reynolds probably won't shed a tear when she learns of her husband's death.

"His wife was notified a little while ago when she arrived at the courthouse for the trial. That's why we couldn't notify you sooner. We had to notify the next of kin first," the sheriff explains.

"What did he use to hang himself?"

"It appears he used a bed sheet."

"It appears?"

"We've opened an investigation."

"Is that standard?"

"Yes. Anytime there is a death, there is an investigation."

"So why did you say it appears he used a bed sheet? Either he used a sheet to hang himself or he didn't."

The Sheriff folded his arms across his chest as though the move would intimidate me. It did not. "The death of Evan Reynolds is under investigation. That's all the information we're prepared to release at this time."

Chapter 24
Michael

Kate and I stare at the television screen in total
disbelief. Today is only Sunday, but Friday evening's
interview with Brigida feels like a lifetime ago. On
Saturday, Senator Tenney, leaders of the local chapter
of the NAACP, and members of the Black Lives
Matter movement concluded their protests with a rally
held in the historic Marshall Park. Marshall Park has
been a frequent location for protests in the past. With
monuments to both The Holocaust and Martin Luther
King Jr, the park is serene and provides a beautiful
relaxing view of the city. The day was peaceful even
though the leaders of the protest basically called for
Ron's head on a platter. There were thousands of
teenagers in the park carrying signs with pictures of

Khalil Jeffries. Khalil's parents spoke to reporters through their tears and told how their hopes for their son's future died when Ron took Khalil's life. Senator Tenney called for the voters of North Carolina to demand their State Representatives push for stricter sentencing when there is a history of violence in the offender's past. He slammed the DA, Landon McMurray, for allowing Ron's case to be rushed through the system without proper time to conduct a full investigation. In his worse and most damning allegation, Senator Tenney boldly blamed the Governor of North Carolina for appointing a young judge with little to no experience to hear such life altering cases. He placed what he labeled as a personal insult and another blemish on the record of justice, on the Governor's shoulders. The accusations were strong and currently being replayed over and over via news sound bites.

The evening, as it often happens in these types of situations, took a much darker tone. Ron's building, along with many of the other beautiful businesses downtown, was destroyed after rioters took to the streets to show their displeasure over Ron's suspended sentence. Several fires were set during the hours it took for the Charlotte Mecklenburg Police Department to restore order. Pictures of the damage splash across the television screen as Kate gasps and covers her mouth with her hand.

"Oh my God Michael. I can't believe you are a part of all of this destruction!"

"What? How the hell can you blame me for this?"

"I told you it wasn't a good idea to accept this case. I knew Ron wasn't telling you everything. A man doesn't beat someone to death without having some type of history of violence in his past."

"Kate, I've known Ron nearly my whole life. I've never known him to even raise his voice, let alone his hands to anyone."

"That's my point Michael! You were blind to who Ron truly is. You believed everything he said without doing your due diligence on him. He killed two children and you just rushed to help him get off."

"Ron didn't get off! He plead guilty. He's a convicted felon at this point! Justice was served!"

"Justice for whom? Michelle? Khalil Jeffries? You actually think a slap on the wrist suspended sentence is justice for killing two teenagers? What if it were our son someone beat to a bloody pulp? Would you be so quick to listen to someone go on and on about what a good man that person was?"

"You're forgetting that one of those teenagers killed was Ron's own daughter! He'll have to live with that for the rest of his life! He killed his own kid. Isn't that punishment enough?"

"How does that help Khalil Jeffries' parents Michael? They'll never get to see their son graduate, or go off to college. They'll never see him get married or have children."

"That's not my fault Kate! What the hell was I supposed to do, watch the man that practically raised me spend the rest of his life in prison?"

"That's the point! You keep talking about Ron! You're forgetting about the victims! Their lives were taken and all you want to focus on is Ron."

"I don't understand you Kate," I say as I stand and begin pacing around the room. "Every other day you're complaining that I don't care enough about the clients. You're always harping on how the poor and innocent need counsel. Ron may be rich, but he..."

"He's not innocent Michael! He's a murderer. He nearly beat Sean Tenney to death 30 years ago and now he's succeeded two times over. Two innocent lives have been taken and you keep trying to turn Ron into the victim!"

"I never said he was a victim, but he's not a monster either. Am I not supposed to defend him because he's rich? I told you Kate, I'm not the bleeding-heart socialist that you are. I have money! I defend people who have money! Ron was there for me when I was a lonely kid with parents who only cared when I did something they didn't like. You may not like him, but Ron deserves the same defense as everyone else."

"Funny, I never heard you fight for poor clients like this," Kate says with a venom that stings me.

"I almost died fighting for Shamika! I literally defended that girl with my life!"

"Who's gonna defend the lives of Michelle and Khalil?"

"Are you freaking kidding me right now? Kate! We're defense attorneys. If you're having some sort of attack of conscious right now, you need to deal with that. It's our job to defend the clients, not the victims."

"I can't do this with you Michael. I thought I could. I thought I could just assimilate to Ayers & Ayers and still maintain who I am, but you make that impossible. I can't work with someone who so readily defends murderers and shows no remorse when it's revealed the man has a history of violence. Where's your heart?"

Kate breaks down into tears as a nurse rushes into the room. It takes a moment for me to grasp that we were yelling. On a quiet Sunday morning in a hospital, while my wife's body is battling to hold on to our son, I got into a full-fledged yelling match with her that left her in tears. I hang my head feeling like I've hit rock bottom. I don't bother saying goodbye as I grab my shoes, wallet, keys, and cell phone before heading out of the room. I see the eyes of the staff staring at me as I leave the hospital. The accusations in their eyes fuels my anger and disappointment with myself. Once safely inside the elevator and away from their judgment, I pull my phone from my pocket and text Nadine. I'm angry with her too, but I know she'll be there for my wife. Regardless of how hurt and angry I am, I love my wife and our unborn son. I need to know someone who loves them is looking after them, even if that person can't be me.

Chapter 25
Ryan

I don't know why I came to the office on a Sunday. Maybe I still feel awkward at home with Janice, or maybe the guilt of Evan's suicide is slowly choking the life out of me; I can't be sure which one is correct. Either way, I need to find something, anything to focus on to escape the prison of my own mind.

There's something eerily serene about being in the office alone. Walking the halls without the obligatory nods and smiles at people whose names I can't remember brings about a euphoric freedom that I can't quite explain. The silence of the office gives me time and space to plot my next move and begin researching my next cases. I technically have not been assigned to anything else, but I'm sure I can find something to work on in Kate's office. I've spent almost as much time in her office as I have my own, so I know where she keeps her files and which cases mean the most to her. Getting a jumpstart on a new case is exactly what I need to move forward and retain my sanity.

Hours later, I'm surrounded by files on Kate's floor when a deep voice booms and startles me.

"What the hell are you doing in here?"

I look up and see an angry Michael staring down at me.

"I'm sorry. I just needed something to work on to clear my head so I came in here to start on some of Kate's cases."

"How long have you been here?"

"I don't know...a couple hours I guess," I say as Michael walks into the room. He's upright and walking straight but I can tell he's had a few drinks. For a moment, I'm taken aback by the sight of my boss under the influence in the office, but I figure with all he has going on, we should consider ourselves fortunate he isn't stone cold drunk during normal business hours. I want to know why he's here at the office and not at the hospital with Kate, but I know better than to ask. With all that Janice and I are going through, I'm no longer surprised by anything that happens between a husband and wife.

"Sorry to hear about your client," Michael says as he plops down on the floor next to me.

The clear liquor splashes in the bottle he's carrying and catches my attention. Michael watches my eyes travel to the bottle and offers it to me without a word. I know I should refrain. I know I shouldn't be drinking at the office, with my boss of all people, but I take the bottle and turn it up to my lips and welcome the burning sensation as the liquid salve travels down to my empty belly.

"The worse part about it is, I can't blame the guy. I saw it coming."

"How?" Michael asks as he takes the bottle back from me before I'm ready to let it go.

"When Thomas first sandbagged me with this case, I wanted nothing to do with it. I have a daughter. I'd die before I hurt her. I thought any man who let his daughter drown deserved to die in prison. Then I met

Evan and I saw the kind of despair and regret only a father could understand. Nothing the courts could do would be worse than what he'd already done to himself. I remember telling my wife if anything happened to our daughter on my watch I'd kill myself before sundown, but it never occurred to me to ask for Evan to be put on suicide watch."

I reach for the bottle again, but something in Michael's face has changed. I pull my empty hand back to my lap, but do not break our eye contact. His red rimmed eyes are locked in on me. I squirm slightly under his gaze unsure of what I've said to disrupt the moment, but I hold my ground. If he's trying to intimidate me, it won't work.

"What did you mean when you said Thomas sandbagged you? Why'd you use that phrase?"

I release the breath I didn't know I was holding. "Thomas barely spoke to me in all of the time I worked for him. Then out of the blue he's waiting for me in my office telling me I'm the man for Evan's case."

"Wait...Thomas was in your office? He didn't call you to his?"

"That's exactly my point! Everyone knows how egomaniacal he is. He doesn't come to us and pass out compliments when he assigns cases."

"Did you ask him why he picked you?"

"Yeah and he tried to feed me some line about everyone having to handle the tough cases now that Kate was gone. I knew it was bullshit the moment it left his lips."

Michael stares out pensively for a moment. "And Evan never had any other priors?"

"No. He hasn't even had a traffic ticket in ages."

"Then why his case? What reason would Thomas have to assign you specifically to the case?"

"I don't know for sure, but I have a hunch. I got so caught up in Evan and my own personal stuff that I didn't have time to really dig into it."

"What's the hunch?"

"I don't know the extent of the connection, but Tanya and Lisa Reynolds are old friends."

"Tanya? What does she have to do with Thomas assigning you to the case?"

I chuckle slightly at Michael's ignorance. "Thomas and Tanya are having an affair. It's been going on for years."

Michael's face twists into a disgusted expression. He closes his eyes and shutters. Despite the heaviness of the mood, I burst into laughter. The vision of Thomas and Tanya is too much for most people to handle. Tanya is known for her flirting, but most men I know are not remotely close to being interested. She's not really unattractive, but she's tall and slightly frightening. Her personality is even larger than her body which is no easy feat. I'm certain her hands are large enough to palm a basketball and the old cuts on her face have left deep lines that her makeup creeps into throughout the day. The idea of Tanya in all of her glory rolling around in the sheets with Thomas' equally large rapidly aging frame is off putting to say the least.

"So, you think Tanya used her influence over Thomas to get you assigned to the case of her friend's husband?" Michael questions after we both recover.

"That doesn't make sense. Lisa should want her husband to have the best defense possible."

"Not if she hates him. She wanted nothing to do with defending him. She nearly attacked me the first time I tried to talk to her about the case."

"Something isn't adding up here."

"I know, but I haven't been able to put the pieces together. I spoke to Higgins, but so far he hasn't been able to find anything."

"Because he may not have been looking for the right thing," Michael says as he stands and goes to the desk phone. He lifts the receiver and dials numbers.

"Higgins, I need you to come to the office as soon as possible and bring everything you have on the case Ryan asked you to look into." There's a short pause before Michael continues. "Yes, I know it's Sunday. Get here now."

I sit watching as Michael jumps into work mode. I have no idea what he's thinking, but for the first time I realize I have a front row seat to one of the greatest legal maneuverers Charlotte has ever seen. Whatever he's about to do is going to be something for the history books.

Chapter 26
Michael

It takes Higgins a full hour to get to the office, but when he does, the three of us turn the conference room into a war room. Higgins lays out the information he's uncovered as Ryan and I listen closely.

"On the morning of the death of baby Ciara, Lisa Reynolds reported to work at Novant Health around 7:30. She had to be on-time because she'd already been written up for being late too many times. According to one of her co-workers, she not only comes in late, but she usually goes missing at some point throughout the day. She works in the janitorial department cleaning the patients' rooms. On the day of the baby's death, Lisa was found crying in one of the empty rooms. She wouldn't tell anyone what was wrong, but the girl I interviewed said she remembered looking for Lisa for over an hour before they found her."

"How can the co-worker be sure it was the day the baby died?"

"Because Lisa missed a week of work after the baby died. The day they found her crying was the last day she worked, so that would mean it was the day she found her baby in the sink."

"I saw Lisa Reynolds that week," Ryan chimed in. "She was wearing scrubs like she'd been to work."

Higgins grins. "That's where the story gets interesting. I have a buddy that works in security at the hospital. He lets me peak at the security footage if I slip him a couple dollars. The video footage from the day the baby died is missing. It's been deleted from the hard drive."

"How is that even possible?"

"Mike, with the right connections anything can be deleted from anywhere," Higgins responds before continuing his explanation. "Someone deleted the entire day's footage along with half a day's footage three days later. They messed up though,"

"How so?" Ryan asks.

"The footage was deleted on-site, not remotely. The hospital has high tech firewalls to prevent hacking. Only a serious network security genius would be able to get around them remotely. But...at the hospital, it is much easier to gain access to the servers. The problem with deleting the footage on-site is there isn't really a way to delete your exit. A person with firsthand knowledge of the camera locations may be able to escape without being discovered, but unfortunately for Lisa, she forgot about exterior cameras."

"You mean she went through all that and forgot to dodge the parking lot cameras?" I question with genuine confusion. I know criminals aren't always the smartest individuals, but it seems someone capable of erasing security footage from a server should be smart enough to avoid being captured leaving the facility.

"No, that part was dumb luck. The Charlotte Mecklenburg Police Department had one of those crime vans across the street. Apparently, there have been problems with people breaking into cars parked on the street. I got our old friend Detective Jennings to pull the footage and there's a clear shot of Lisa Reynolds leaving the hospital minutes after the second security black out."

"What would she have to gain from deleting the security footage?" I ask still not connecting the dots.

"Shit! Kate was right," Ryan yells as he runs out of the conference room.

Higgins and I look at each other in confusion until the young lawyer comes back to the room waving a stack of papers.

"While Kate and I were preparing Evan's defense, she noticed an inconsistency in the report. Higgins, what time did the first security footage go black?"

Higgins looks back through his notes. "11am."

"And what time did the co-worker say she found Lisa crying?"

"She said it was after lunch, around 1pm."

Ryan walks to the whiteboard and draws a timeline. "Lisa said in her statement to the police that she left

her house at 7am. On her way out the door, she woke
Evan and told him to finish feeding their daughter who
was crying uncontrollably. That would mean shortly
after 7am, Evan would have fed the baby and
accidentally put her in the sink, but the medical
examiner's report said the time of death was around
noon. If the security footage went black around 11am,
Lisa Reynolds could have snuck out of the hospital,
drove home and drowned her daughter, then make it
back to the hospital before the co-worker found her
crying at 1."

"What would be her motive?"

"That's the problem Kate and I had. From what we
could tell, Lisa was a great mother. She'd already raised
three children and there were never any abuse claims."

"But she did suffer from postpartum depression with
her third baby," Higgins said, taking command of the
conversation again. "Don't ask me how I got this
information because you don't want to know. Just
promise me you'll defend me if I ever need it."

The small joke is rare coming from Higgins, but I
welcome it. "If you need an attorney, I'll personally

defend you without hesitation. I owe you," I say honestly.

Higgins walks over the white board and adds his evidence to Ryan's. "Lisa Reynolds was treated for postpartum depression for two years following the birth of her third child. She even became pregnant during the course of the treatment. She was afraid she wouldn't be able to handle another child, so she had an abortion without telling Evan."

"Are you sure Evan didn't know?" Ryan questions.

"I'm certain. I found old emails she sent to her cousin saying Evan would kill her if he ever found out she aborted their baby."

Ryan and I both take a moment to soak in everything Higgins is saying. A mother suffering from postpartum depression years ago still doesn't add up to murder. There's still a piece of the puzzle missing. How does Lisa jump from one extreme to the other? And how could Evan not have known his wife was suffering so deeply?

Higgins smiles at Ryan and me. "I can see both of your wheels turning, but you still haven't asked me the million dollar question."

"What did we miss?" I ask.

"You didn't ask me who her cousin is."

Chapter 27
Ryan

Michael and I stare at Higgins as the answer to the riddle comes to us simultaneously. I knew Tanya and Lisa were old friends. The thought of the two of them being related never crossed my mind. Another thought occurs to me just as quickly.

"Were you able to find a connection to Thomas? He had to know something. He put me on this case hoping my love for my own daughter would make me hate Evan for killing his. Plus he was banking on my lack of experience. That's why he fired me when I got Kate to come on board as lead counsel."

"I'm still digging, but I have Tanya's cell phone records. I'm still tracing most of the numbers, but she made several calls to the same numbers which brings me to my next point. I know you didn't ask me to

Michael, but I've been doing some digging into the Ron Edahl case."

Michael's interest in the conversation grows even more intense. "How could Thomas be tied to Ron? To my knowledge, they've never met."

"I saw Tanya on some of the news footage standing behind Khalil's mother, Leona. When she popped up in this case, my gut told me there was something there. Did you ever wonder how Sean Tenney heard about Ron's case and organized so quickly?"

"Of course I did. I saw Tanya in the courtroom the day Ron was sentenced. We fired her immediately, but I haven't had time to dig into the connection. Hell, I didn't even know about her and Thomas until today. If I had known she never would have worked for me."

Higgins laughs loudly. "How could you not know? She falls all over him every chance she gets."

"She falls all over everyone. How was I supposed to know Thomas would be the type of man to fall for a woman like that?"

"A woman like that?" Higgins teases with a raised eyebrow.

"Don't even try it," Michael shot back. "You have eyes. You know exactly what I mean. Now get to the point. What does Tanya have to do with Sean Tenney?"

"I'm still working on that, but Tanya's cell records indicate she and Leona Jeffries have been communicating regularly for weeks. There were also several calls to reporters."

"So that's how the media got wind of Michelle's memorial service. Tanya tipped them off."

"But what good does that do her?" I question.

"It's not her. Can't you see? Tanya is a pawn. This is all Thomas' doing," Michael says through clinched teeth.

Thomas Willoughby has been the Public Defender for years. He's served his office well, or so it's seemed. I actually had respect for the guy even after he freaked out because Michael hired Kate away from him. I never understood his disdain for Michael after he returned to Ayers & Ayers. It's not as though they're competitors. Thomas manages a public office that has to help any defendant who can't afford counsel, Michael is the managing partner of a firm that caters to high end clientele. I thought they'd developed a bond during the time Michael worked for him, but Thomas quickly released Michael following Bruce Ayers' death. This thought causes another one to jump in my mind and I inwardly curse myself for not catching it sooner.

"Higgins," I say with urgency. "I need you to dig into the history between Michael's father and Thomas. And I need you to do it quickly. If we can find what I think we can find, we can end the protests and get the city of Charlotte back on track immediately.

It's now after 5pm on a Sunday, the day where Janice, Kaitlin, and I are supposed to be sitting down for family dinner with Janice's parents. I've missed every dinner since Janice's admission, so one more shouldn't matter much. In talking with Michael and Higgins, we uncovered several links, but not enough to connect them all together. There's still one very big question sitting at the base of my skull, nagging the hell out of me.

I pull into the jail's parking lot and rush inside. I walk up to the one person that I know will level with me.

"Hey Harvey."

"Hey Ry-man! What's going on? You working Sunday's now?" Harvey is his usually excited and jovial self. I hate to drop all of this on him and ruin his day, but he's my last chance at putting all of this together.

"Yeah man, they pulled me in on a Sunday."

"Who you here to see?" Harvey asks without letting me finish what I wanted to say.

"I actually need to see you. You got a break coming up?"

Harvey looks apprehensive, but nods to the bailiff working with him. "Hey, hold it down till I get back. If anybody asks where I am, tell em I went to take a dump." Harvey laughs to lighten the comment, but the sound is forced and I can easily tell he knows what I want to talk to him about. He follows me outside and we hop in my car to talk in private.

"What do you know Harvey?"

"Who says I know anything?"

"You do, with the way you're acting. In all the times I've been here, I've never asked to speak with you privately. When I do, you readily come out here, which means you knew I was coming. What's going on?"

"What they did to your boy wasn't right."

"What who did?"

"Look, I'll give you the info because it wasn't right, but you can't let this come back on me. If they're willing to kill, nothing will stop them from killing my black ass. I got a wife and three kids that need me, so keep my name out this shit."

"Done. Now tell me who you're talking about."

"Thomas Willoughby and the dead man's wife. I don't know her name but I recognized her from TV."

"Tell me everything!"

***

It was well after 8 pm when I finally pulled into the garage. After talking to Harvey, I drove around trying to wrap my mind around what he'd told me. Not only was it hard for me to believe Thomas was capable of what Harvey said, but I couldn't believe I didn't see the truth sooner. Thomas was planning this all along. He gambled on my inexperience, but this was one bet he was going to lose.

I walk in the house and drop my keys into the bowl by the door. The downstairs is dark and I silently curse myself for missing Kaitlin's bedtime yet again. I haven't spent nearly enough time with my daughter recently. I flick on the kitchen light and nearly yell when I see Janice sitting at the kitchen island.

"Janice! What the hell are you doing sitting in here in the dark?"

"I came down when I heard the garage door."

"Well why didn't you turn on a light? You almost gave me a heart attack," I complain as I head to the fridge and grab a bottle of water.

"We need to talk Ryan."

"Not this shit again Janice! We're just starting to get back on the right track. Don't mess it up again."

"There's nothing to mess up! You never really let us recover from me telling you about Clifton."

"Don't say his name in my house! Don't ever say his fucking name to me again!"

"See! That's what I'm talking about! You're not letting it go!"

"Janice, I'm trying," I say a little softer. "It's not that simple to just forget my wife was falling for someone else."

"But it's easy to forget your daughter?"

"What are you talking about? I never forgot my daughter!"

"Ryan are you kidding me? You've been gone all day! You left before she got up which is strange considering getting you out of bed is nothing short of a miracle every damn day, but all of a sudden today, of all days, you're up and out of the house before 8am! Then you don't show up until after she's cried herself to sleep. What the hell is wrong with you? Punish me...I get it, but I draw the line at Kaitlin. I won't let her spend another night crying herself to sleep because her Daddy forgot about her."

"Stop saying that! I didn't forget about my daughter! My client killed himself on Friday! I've been working all damn day and I won't let you make me feel guilty for it."

"It's her birthday you self-absorbed son of a bitch! You're knee deep in a dead man who killed his daughter and forgot your own living breathing daughter's birthday! I called you at least 20 times! I left you voicemails! I texted you! Ignore me.... fine! If you want out of this marriage, you know where the door is, but don't you ever ignore my daughter again! Either get your shit together Ryan or get the fuck out! Kaitlin and I will be better off without you, than having you hang around here half-assing your responsibilities as a husband and father."

I hang my head as Janice storms out of the kitchen. I'm pissed at her tone and the effrontery of her accusations. I want to yell back at her. I want to accuse her of attacking me to get the heat off of her for what she's done. However, no matter how painful it is for me to admit it, I know she's right. There's no excuse for me forgetting my daughter's birthday. What makes this feel worse is, I now understand how Evan could be living with his wife and not see how troubled she was. I didn't even know my own wife was feeling ignored, yet I judged Evan for the same thing. I feel like the worst type of hypocrite. It's so easy to get caught up in work and providing for my wife and daughter financially. It's easy to feel like a hero when I kill a bug, change a light bulb, reach something on a high shelf, or carry heavy bags from the car. Those are the things I think about, the things expected of a man. All along, my wife and daughter needed more than my muscle, they needed my heart to protect theirs.

Chapter 28
Michael

I hear their voices before I see their faces and the smile that spreads across my face reaches from ear to ear. I walk into Kate's room and my heart wells with love. My wife is surrounded by Nadine, Shamika, Syreeta, and little Adrian. The women are chatting and laughing effortlessly while Adrian plays with a truck in his mother's arms. It's hard to believe how much my former client has grown and matured since she's been living with Syreeta, her birth mother. Their relationship hasn't been perfect, but the two are healing and growing together now that the people who changed the course of their lives are both dead. Shamika is no longer the scared teenager who wouldn't speak or stand up for herself. Now she's a confident college student and loving mother. After negotiating their financial settlements, I worried that having more money than either of them ever dreamed of may do more harm than good. I'm grateful Syreeta and Shamika both proved me wrong. They've stuck to their wealth management classes and have followed the advice of the financial planner down to the smallest details. Shamika reminds me of the good in the world and I instantly feel a pang of guilt. In many ways Kate is right, the Shamikas of the world are the ones that need my help, not people like Ron who can afford to hire any high-powered attorney. I already have more money than one person will need in a lifetime. It's time for me to really evaluate who I am as a man and soon-to-be father. I didn't admit it to Kate because it really stung, but her point about our son was spot on. If anyone ever hurt my child, I wouldn't care about any previous good that person had done. As much as I hate to think about it, I have to acknowledge to myself that a decision must be made concerning Ayers & Ayers.

"You guys didn't tell me you were having a party," I say breaking into the conversation.

"Michael!" Shamika exclaims and she leaps to her feet with Adrian still in her arms. She rushes over and gives me a hug that turns the three of us into a loose sandwich with Adrian acting as the meat. It only lasts a second, but I feel like a father when she hugs me, and again a sharp pain shoots through my heart.

"Hey everybody. It's good to see you Shamika," I say while smiling through my pain and rubbing her toddler's back.

"I was hoping we'd get to see you before we left. You're always so busy. We never get to see you anymore."

"I know Sweetie, but all of that is changing soon." I look directly at Kate while delivering the news to Shamika. I need Kate to read between the lines.

Kate returns my stare, but her expression is hard. I don't see the love in her eyes that normally makes me weak in the knees. I don't know what to make of it. I can't be sure if she's falling out of love with me or if she's still pissed about our fight. I'm hoping it's the latter.

"Michael, I know you just got here and you're anxious to visit with everyone, but can I steal you away for a second?" Nadine asks as she stands and shows me she isn't waiting for a response.

Since she's not really giving me a choice, I don't bother responding. I follow Nadine to the hallway expecting her to stop outside of Kate's door. Instead she keeps walking towards the elevators.

"Nadine, where are we going?"

"To talk. This is going to take some time and I'm too old to stand out here. Let's go grab a cup of coffee downstairs. I've been silent far too long."

Nadine wastes no time digging into me after we take our seats. "Michael, I'm not going to sugar coat this for you. I'm too old to beat around bushes, and quite frankly I've never been good at it. If you don't straighten up you're going to lose your wife."

I'm not at all shocked by Nadine's direct tone or her words. "I know."

"You know? Then what the hell are you doing? You actually got into an argument with her while she's hospitalized to give your child the best chance at survival? Don't you know stress can throw her into preterm labor?"

"I know! I wasn't trying to upset her. I lost my cool when she blamed me for the riots. How the hell could she point fingers at me?"

"Because you let yourself get so blinded by the case that you turned into someone we barely recognized. You willingly defended a man that killed two children with his bare hands. You wouldn't listen to reason. You were returning to that same arrogant, out of touch jerk we all loathed and there was nothing anyone could do to stop you. You snapped at anyone who tried to get you to even consider any other alternatives."

"That's not fair! I wasn't being a jerk. I was trying to do my job! I'm a defense attorney. Every client isn't going to be a poor, down and out kid that needs saving. Sometimes the client isn't all that likeable, but they still deserve a proper defense. I still have to do the right thing even when my wife thinks it's the wrong client."

"No one is blaming you for doing your job Michael. You're a damn good attorney. Kate loves that about you. The problem is, you can't see the opportunity you're sitting on. You're a bit of a local celebrity, and you have the financial resources to really make a positive impact. And I'm not just talking about here in Charlotte. You can change the world Michael. Instead of seizing the opportunity, you choose to represent the same wealthy clients. Your status and wealth afford you something most people will never really experience, the freedom of choice."

My shoulders drop as the weight of Nadine's words settle within me. They are an unwelcomed addition to the pain and disappointment already residing there. I take a long swig of coffee and enjoy the bitter sting as it distracts me from the stinging in my chest. "I know you're right Nadine. I didn't look into Ron's past because I trusted him. I thought I knew enough to jump right into the case. That wasn't the best idea, but I'm not sad I took his case. Ron doesn't belong in prison. Call me an elitist all you want, but Ron adds value to society by running his company and creating jobs. Putting him behind bars won't bring Khalil Jeffries back and everyone working for him would lose their jobs if his company folds. Do you know what that would do to our local economy if hundreds of people are suddenly without jobs? Charlotte is finally recovering from the recession. Ron and his company's acquisitions played a huge role in that recovery. He's made his share of mistakes. I can admit that. He manipulated the system, but he's not a monster. Patty and I may be the only people alive that still believe in him, but I can't forget the love and guidance he showed me when no one else cared. A lot of the good you and Kate see in me came from Ron and Patty. There was no way I could have stood by and let them go through the worst time of their lives alone."

"Remember, even the worst tyrants in history showed love to someone. Ron loving you doesn't excuse the wrong he's done."

"I know that and I'm trying to figure out what I'm going to do. I can't promise I'll never defend anyone else like Ron, unless..." I pause, unsure if I can even say the words aloud.

"Unless what?" Nadine urges.

"Unless I close the firm and walk away from it all."

Nadine doesn't bother hiding her surprise. "I can't lie, I'm shocked. You love being an attorney."

"I loved trying to be the man my father wanted me to be. I'm not sure I ever really took the time to figure out what I wanted. I want to be someone my wife and son can be proud of. I don't know if I can be that man and keep Ayers & Ayers open."

"This might actually be a good thing."

I'm not sure what Nadine is getting at. How could closing the firm my father built from the ground up be a good thing? "Why would you say that?"

It's Nadine's turn to take a long swig of coffee to prolong her response. "I promised Kate I wouldn't tell you, but this has gone on long enough."

I straighten my back at the thought that Nadine knows something about my wife that I don't. Kate and I promised to never keep secrets from one another, now Nadine is about to tell me my wife has broken that promise. Nadine immediately senses the change in my demeanor.

"Relax Michael. She's been dealing with it since before the two of you got married. I'm the only one that knows besides the therapist that diagnosed her."

"Therapist? What the hell are you talking about Nadine?"

"Have you wondered why Kate overreacted to this case?"

"Of course I have. I guessed it was the pregnancy hormones. She's always been passionate about her work. I figured the baby pushed her over the edge."

"As usual, you have all of the emotional perception of a rock. Kate is suffering from compassion fatigue."

I try to recall where I've heard that term before. The memory is just beyond my reach, but I'm close.

"People who care for trauma victims can experience it. It was initially diagnosed in nurses."

"That's it! I attended a lecture a couple years ago that focused on the warning signs in lawyers. Kate doesn't fit any of the signs."

"She does Michael. What you see is her fighting to hang on to her ability to feel. Haven't you noticed how over the top she is when she talks about the innocent?"

"Yes. It's all she cares about. She goes on and on about making sure the innocent aren't railroaded."

"Have you really not noticed how her voice goes hollow? She's saying the words, but she doesn't mean them. Kate hates the fact that her heart won't let her feel the way she used to. She pretends to feel empathy, compassion, anger even, when the truth is she feels nothing. Kate is a fantastic attorney, but she was too emotionally invested. No one could go on like that forever, so her mind began protecting her by cutting off her access to her own compassion."

"That doesn't make sense. I've seen her break down in tears just reading about cases. Kate cares more than anyone I know."

"No. You've seen Kate break down crying because she can't feel as deeply as she used to. A piece of her broke after the experience with that teenager Davion. She's never really recovered. She's been hanging on by a thread. I'm afraid she's going to have a mental breakdown if she doesn't take a break."

"Nadine, I live with her. I'd know if she was faking her emotions."

"No you wouldn't, because you don't know what she was like before Davion."

"And neither do you," I challenge.

"Touché, but you're forgetting who I am and what I've spent my life doing. As a social worker, I've seen any and everything you can think of. I used to be Kate. I think that's why we hit it off that first night you brought her to my house. I saw some of my younger self. I saw the good and the bad. I knew she was suffering that first night, but it wasn't until she moved in with me that I became worried."

I try to calm my rapidly rising temper. I don't know if I'm pissed at Kate for keeping her struggle from me or Nadine for helping her hide it. I'm her husband. I'm the first person she should have come to. Instead, she's been confiding in Nadine and keeping me in the dark. She's been pretending with me just like with everyone else. I'm angry, but even worse, I'm hurt. I don't know my wife nearly as well as I thought I did.

"Cool your jets Michael," Nadine starts again. "She couldn't tell you when she was in denial herself. Kate insists she's fine, but I can spot compassion fatigue a mile away. I've seen too many social workers pretend to care long after their hearts turned cold. No one can see the worst society has to offer day in and day out without being affected. Some go quietly into the dark hole of hopelessness, others are like Kate. They force smiles on their faces and try to pretend nothing has changed when they're completely disconnected from their emotions. What makes Kate unique is that she's trying to fight it. She wants to feel. She wants to remain in touch with her emotions. The problem is, her heart and mind can't take it, so they are fighting to protect her from herself."

I sigh and run my fingers through my hair. I thought I'd beat this nervous tick, but it still pops up during moments of intense stress. Hearing my wife is struggling with a secondary traumatic stress condition definitely qualifies as a moment of intense stress. What makes this moment worse is that I've been so preoccupied with Ron that I missed the signs of her unraveling. I'm now wondering how much of Kate moving in with Nadine was about me and how much was about what she was dealing with.

"Nadine, when she left me, was that about me or what she's dealing with?"

"A little bit of both. I think she's afraid staying married to you will push her deeper into her condition. You have the ability to disconnect without detaching your emotions. Kate's afraid if she picks up that habit, she'll never be able to turn her compassion back on. She's terribly stressed out about it Michael, which is why you need to do everything in your power not to add any extra stress."

"If I had a clue about any of this I would have done things much differently. I can't fix things if she won't even tell me there's a problem."

"She doesn't want you to try to fix her Michael. I'm not even sure if she knows what she wants right now. And quite frankly, I think it's too stressful for her to try to figure out. She needs to rest so your son can stay put a little longer. I know this is going to be hard for you, but it would be in Kate's best interest for you not to say anything about this until after the baby is born."

"I agree. Besides...I have no idea what to say or do. I need time to process all of this. Plus I have to deal with some things. Which reminds me, I need to ask you some hard questions about your friend Thomas."

"Thomas?"

"Yes. I need to know that I can trust you not to repeat anything I'm saying to you. I know you two are close and I'm not trying to put you in the middle, but I need answers."

"I don't know how much help I'll be."

"Why is that?"

"Thomas and I stopped being friends the moment he asked me to choose between the two of you."

"When did that happen?"

"Shortly after your father died."

"It seems Thomas drew his battle lines then, and I was the only one who wasn't notified. Do you know the history between Thomas and my father?"

"I don't know the specifics, but I know there was bad blood. I was very shocked when Thomas told me you were working for him. Then when your father died and released all of that footage, I assumed your father must have had something on him too. I thought you knew."

I throw my head back in laughter at the irony of the situation. I've had the ammunition to put an end to Thomas' shenanigans all this time and didn't even realize it. "Nadine I could kiss you right now," I say as I leap up from the table and run out of the room. "Tell Kate I'll be back as soon as possible," I yell over my shoulder before I round the corner.

Chapter 29
Ryan

Waking up in the guest room still feels strange. I barely slept a wink so when the sun peeped in through the blinds, my eyes popped wide awake. I don't think I ever entered deep sleep last night. My head is pounding. My mouth is dry, and my legs feel weighted. Despite all of that, I drag my body in the direction of my daughter's voice. When I walk out of the guest room, Kaitlin and Janice's backs are turned to me. The two of them are engrossed in a conversation about blueberries and I stand there not wanting to interrupt their moment. For what it's worth, Janice is still the most beautiful woman I've ever met and no matter what mistake she made, I don't want to spend another night like last night. It's hard to admit I played a part in her mistake, but I did. She's bent over backwards for me for years and in return I've taken her for granted.

"Good morning. How are Daddy's favorite girls today?"

"Daddy!" Kaitlin squeals as she leaves her mother and runs to me. My daughter who rations out hugs like food during a famine, is hugging me like her little life depends on it. I close my eyes and enjoy the moment. I needed this just as much as she did. I open my eyes and see Janice watching us. Her eyes are full of tears as I walk over to her and add her to the hug. The three of us stand there together, healing and appreciating like we never have before, and the importance of giving these two the best of me sinks down into my soul.

"I won't let you two down again," I whisper as we silently exchange our love.

***

After a long breakfast with Janice and Kaitlin, I dress and head to the office. There are reporters and news vans everywhere, a response to the rioting over the weekend no doubt. Ron Edahl and Evan Reynolds are the leading news stories on every local station as well as a few national ones. With the information I got from Harvey, along with Higgins' intel, Michael and I should be able to bring the truth to light for both stories. I head straight for Michael's office and take a seat while he finishes his phone call.

"You're not going to believe what I uncovered after we left yesterday."

"I bet I can top it, but you go first," Michael says with a rare smile.

"I have an informant at the jail that swears Thomas and Lisa Reynolds snuck in to see Evan late Thursday night."

"Why would Thomas allow himself to be seen with Lisa?"

"Apparently Thomas has been making late night visits to the jail for years. The whole night shift is paid to keep quiet, but my informant was asked to work a double at the last minute. He wasn't supposed to be able to see them, but he snuck away for a little while. When he was returning he saw Thomas and Lisa going inside."

"Is he willing to testify?"

"No. He's afraid he'll be killed. He's convinced Thomas and Lisa killed Evan. He says there's no way Evan could have hung himself without someone intervening. He swears Evan hung himself with a belt, not a sheet like the Sheriff said. Inmates aren't allowed to have belts. Thomas would have had to give him one. There's no way to tell what they said to him to push him over the edge, but it couldn't have taken much. Evan was riddled with guilt."

"What would Thomas and Lisa stand to gain by killing Evan?"

"I wondered the same thing. He had no memory of the morning the baby died, but there's evidence that suggests memories can be recovered after the removal of tumors. My theory is they were trying to cover their tracks. They couldn't risk Evan remembering something from that morning. I know we can't prosecute them for encouraging him to kill himself, but just knowing what happened makes me feel a little better."

"We can make sure Lisa's deeds are uncovered."

"What about Thomas?"

"I have a special plan in place for Thomas. He should be receiving notification in about an hour. He has 24 hours to resign and make this Sean Tenney mess disappear or I'll make sure he's never able to show his face in the light of day again."

"What do you have on him?"

"Not me...my father. Bruce Ayers is still speaking from the grave."

I break out in a cheesy grin. Working with Michael is every bit as exciting and invigorating as I thought it would be. The man is a mastermind at this game of power and control. I'm not certain I'm cut out for this lifestyle, but learning directly from Michael is an eye opening experience. "What about Tanya? Is she going to get away with her role in this?"

"You know better than that. I have Higgins working her phone records and a few other angles he uncovered."

Michael reaches into his desk and pulls out a business card that has seen better days. He reaches over the desk and hands me the card. I accept it and read the name aloud. "Detective Jennings. You want me to bring him into the loop?"

"Yes. Jennings and I have history, but he's a good detective. He can't be bought and he won't hesitate to do the right thing. We need him on our side. I'd reach out to him myself, but I need to get back to the hospital."

"No problem. Tell Kate I said hello and I'll get in touch with Jennings."

"Thanks Ryan. And for what it's worth, I'm happy you ignored me and went to Kate for help. We're lucky to have you on board."

"Thanks Michael. That means a lot coming from you."

The meeting with Detective Jennings took place in the art district NoDa. It is an eclectic part of town known for its culturally diverse artistic atmosphere. I've never had a reason to spend time in the area, so I enjoy people watching as I wait for Detective Jennings. He arrives fifteen minutes late and walks straight up to me and starts talking.

"If you and Mike are trying to drag me into your bullshit, you can stop right now. I finally have peace. I'm not gonna have my face all over the papers again messing around with your boss."

"We're not trying to drag you into anything. You're a detective and we have evidence of crimes. We're only trying to help you put criminals behind bars where they belong."

"Don't bullshit me kid. I know Michael, remember? Just tell me what you have."

It takes me a full fifteen minutes to fill Jennings in, but when I'm done he's ready to ask questions.

"So you think Lisa Reynolds murdered her baby and Thomas helped her shame her husband into killing himself to cover her tracks?"

"Yes."

"And how does Tanya fit in?"

"We're not sure. She's Lisa's cousin, but as far as we can tell she wasn't actually involved in hurting the baby and she didn't visit the jail. We were hoping you could fill in the blank there."

"What about Thomas? You guys aren't stupid enough to try to convince me to press charges against the public defender are you?"

I smile at Jennings. "It would be interesting to watch Thomas get arrested and shamed, but no. We have other plans for Thomas."

"Just be careful," Jennings says as he starts to walk away. "Rumor has it Thomas and the mayor are sleeping together. If that's true, he's practically untouchable."

I stand there stunned as Jennings walks away. Thomas is sleeping with the mayor and Tanya? Then it hits me. If what Jennings said is true, we have our way to get Thomas and Tanya to turn on each other.

Two hours later Higgins and I huddle in our makeshift war room again. All information has been removed from the board to prevent my co-workers from seeing what we're working on, but we don't need the timeline. Higgins and I have pieced together enough information to paint a picture we can envision perfectly.

"I have connections at nearly every hotel in the city. No one has seen Thomas in their hotel with anyone.

I've followed him almost every night. He leaves work and goes straight home. I haven't seen anything that suggests an affair with the mayor. Did Jennings say where he heard it?"

"No. You know how rumors are. No one ever knows who started it. What about during office hours? Have you followed him then?"

"No, but I don't think he'd make that type of mistake," Higgins says as he rubs his bald head. "Thomas is smart. He's not going to leave a trail. I'm going to have to dig deeper, but again, if I get caught you or Michael have to help me beat the charge."

"Wait," I say trying to recall the information clearly. "Harvey said Lisa and Thomas went to visit Evan late at night. Maybe that's how you're missing him."

"Say no more. I'm on it."

"What about Tanya? Have you found any evidence against her?"

"I sure did and it's enough to get rid of her and Sean Tenney for good."

"Perfect! Don't tell me now. I want to bring Michael in the loop."

"Bring Michael in the loop on what?" Michael asks as he walks into the conference room.

"What are you doing here? I thought you were going to be at the hospital."

"Kate is resting. I figured I better come back and help you two solve this thing. Take a look at these," Michael says as he drops a manila envelope onto the table.

Higgins and I both jump at the envelope knowing its contents are going to help blow the case wide open. Higgins beats me to it and opens it immediately. He pulls the paper from the envelope and begins examining it. As he finishes each page he passes it to me. I review each page one by one reading through the long lines of names. It takes me a moment to realize what Michael has discovered.

"Where did you get this?"

"From my father."

My quizzical expression made him continue.

"Everyone knows how my father arranged to have information leaked after his death. We've all seen the result of that. Hell, you're sitting here because of it. But what no one knows except Kate and I, well and the two of you now, is that my father left me a safe deposit box that contains more evidence. He didn't tell me who the evidence was against. In the letter he left me he said I'd know when to use everything in the box. I had a talk with Nadine. You know she and Thomas have been friends for a long time, but shortly after my father's death Thomas tried to make her choose between him and me. Of course, Nadine chose me so Thomas hasn't really spoken to her much since. That got me to thinking...what if the real reason Thomas went along with my father's decision to stick me in the public defender's office is because my father had dirt on him too? So I started digging into the files and here we are."

"Higgins has some info on Tanya," I say eager to put all of this to bed.

"I figured out how she got Tenney to come to North Carolina so quickly."

"How?" Michael and I ask in unison.

"Good old-fashion American greed."

Chapter 30
Michael

It's 9am Tuesday morning and my team and I walk into the 4th Street public defender's office like we own the place. Tanya has resumed her post as gate keeper, but a quick word from Detective Jennings and she opens the door and joins us on the elevator. We ride up to the tenth floor and file out one by one as we head straight to Thomas' office. I watch as my former co-workers stare at us in utter disbelief. When we reach Thomas' office Darlene, his secretary, tries her best to stop us, but she's never been very good at keeping me from entering whenever I wanted. There was no way she was going to stop the army marching in this morning.

"Great, I see we're all here," I say with enthusiasm as I enter the office and see Sean Tenney sitting with Thomas.

"Michael, what the hell..." Thomas' voice trails off as he sees the people walking into the office behind me. Ryan, Higgins, Jennings, Landon McMurray, Nadine, and Tanya all file into the office.

Ryan closes the door as I begin speaking. "Sean. I'll deal with you first. I know you're a pawn in all of this, so we're willing to cut you some slack if you issue a statement that clears my client's name, pack up all your race baiting bullshit and go back to Georgia."

Tenney laughs. "And why would I do that."

"Because we have proof that Tanya wired you money to come here and start all of this protest and riot nonsense. I'm sure the voters in Georgia won't be happy to learn their Senator willingly twisted the facts of an old assault case to help a fellow corrupt public servant carry out a personal vendetta. Voters don't readily vote for politicians who can be bought so easily. Besides, this whole scenario is eerily similar to the mess you stirred up in Birmingham. I bet if we dig deep enough we'll find something to prove you manipulated that situation as well."

"I didn't manipulate anything! I fight for the equal rights of people of color. I've dedicated my life to this cause since your client and his friends attacked me! I won't allow you destroying my reputation because I told the truth about your violent, racist client."

It's my turn to laugh. "We figured you say that. If it was so innocent, why the pay-off Tenney?" I smile as Tenney shoots daggers at me with his eyes. Content that his angers proves he knows he's been beaten, I continue the slaughter. "Allow me to introduce you to the district attorney, Landon McMurray. McMurray and I aren't friends, in fact he hates me. But you know what he hates more than me? Corruption, and the chaos and unrest you brought to our city. So, with that in mind, Landon here is prepared to charge you with bribery as well as every crime he can find on the books that will stick. He'll have a news crew out front to watch as Detective Jennings leads you out in handcuffs. You'll make the midday news here and back at home in

Georgia. The choice is yours. Issue the statement and fix this mess you made, or kiss your career goodbye."

"Screw you."

"Is that a yes or no?" I ask enjoying the sight of anger in Tenney's eyes. When he doesn't respond, I fill in the quiet space with my chuckle and most lethal gut punch for him. "If you're thinking of a way out of this, there isn't one. We have the phone records and bank statements. It's clear you're no career criminal because you left a trail of breadcrumbs that would have led a blind man straight to you."

"No, I am not a criminal. I'm only in this mess because I trusted him when he said I had nothing to worry about," Tenney says as he turns his anger towards Thomas.

"Don't worry. He's about to get all the punishment and humiliation he deserves."

"Michael," Thomas says through gritted teeth. "You have exactly one minute to get your spoiled ungrateful ass out of my office before you make me do something I've wanted to do since you first walked in here."

"Save your threats old man. They might have worked in the past, but you don't have a leg to stand on here. Like I said in my email, this is your day of reckoning. Your 24 hours are up."

"You don't get to make demands. I've been an attorney longer than you've been alive! You..."

"I found what my father had on you," I say before Thomas can get wound up into his speech. "So you can save your righteous indignation for someone else. I know the truth about you now."

"You know nothing."

"I know you cheated your way into this office. I know you and the mayor cheated again during the last election. I know you've been sleeping with her, Tanya, *and* Lisa Reynolds. I know you and Lisa Reynolds gave Evan the belt he used to hang himself to cover up the fact that she drowned her baby, not him. Do I need to go on?"

"What the hell is he talking about Thomas?" Tanya yelled from behind me.

I turn to face her. "Hang on Tanya. It's not your turn yet. I have a special surprise for you." I turn my attention back to Thomas. "Now...have you made your decision, or do I need to have Landon here give you a rundown of the penalty for voter fraud which is a Class I felony?"

"Shit," Thomas curses under his breath as he drops down into his chair.

It's odd seeing Thomas cave so easily, but I'm still going to enjoy this moment. "Landon has agreed not to press charges as long as you vacate your office immediately and agree to retire somewhere far away from Charlotte."

"Agreed," Thomas mumbles through tight lips.

"And as for you Tanya," I say as I turn around. "You bribed a Senator and coerced him into creating riotous conditions in the city. There are thousands of dollars worth of damage that the tax payers will have to pay for. And you did it all for a man that's sleeping with your cousin."

"You arrogant son a bitch!" Tanya yells before lunging for me.

I quickly back away as Jennings handcuffs Tanya.

"We can't charge you for the bribe without implicating Senator Tenney, but we can charge you for illegally wiretapping Ayers & Ayers offices."

The look of surprise is priceless as realization that their secret has been revealed. "You make this go away Thomas or I swear I'll tell them everything," Tanya threatens.

Thomas doesn't respond. He just lowers his head as his world falls apart. A knock at the door causes everyone's head to turn in the direction of the sound.

"Ah, just in time," I announce as I squeeze past everyone to open the door. "Mrs. Reynolds, please come in." I step back to allow Lisa Reynolds to enter the room. As soon as she gets a feel for the atmosphere she begins to cry.

"Don't cry now bitch," Tanya hisses. "You weren't crying when you were screwing my man!" Tanya tries to lunge for Lisa, but Jennings' grip is firm on her arms.

I peak my head into the hallway and signal for the two uniformed officers to retrieve Tanya and Lisa.

"Wait!" Tanya yells. "Thomas are you really going to let them take me away like this?"

Again, Thomas remains silent.

"Fine! If that's how you want it, so be it." Tanya turns to face Landon McMurray. "Thomas runs an illegal gambling ring that bets on whether or not defendants will be convicted and he assigns attorneys from this office based on how much he stands to gain from the pot. He's been behind it for years and I have evidence to prove it."

Epilogue
Michael

Kate and I curl up on the sofa with our son Jonah. It's been three weeks since she gave birth and we are enjoying every moment of being his parents. Jonah was born a little early, but thanks to the preventative measures of Kate's doctors, he was able to come home with us a week ago. This has been the greatest time of our lives. I didn't understand the depth of a parent's love until I held my son in my arms for the first time.

I haven't worked a single day in the two and a half months since we took Thomas down and helped restore order to the city. I've spent every day at my wife's side, supporting her in a way I never knew she needed. I never thought I'd enjoy being away from the office, but I do. Ryan is running the day to day operations. He's young and not as experienced as some of the other associates that work for us, but I can trust him to do the right thing. At this stage of my career, I value making the right decision over making more money. It was this line of thought that made me walk away from Ron Edahl as a client.

Ron hired the PR firm Williams & Rollins to repair his image. It's as though the murder of Khalil Jeffries never happened. After the marches and protests ended, after Sean Tenney released his statement, after the damage to downtown was repaired; Khalil Jeffries' memory has been reduced to a social media hashtag.

Ron and I are no longer close. I value everything he was to me in the past, but I realize I've changed in a way that doesn't allow us to remain friends or colleagues. I feel like I repaid the debt I owed him when I helped him with his plan to escape prison time. I tried to ignore the nagging feeling in my gut, but the ease at which Ron was able to manipulate his freedom left a bad taste in my mouth.

Ayers & Ayers is slowly weening away from violent criminal cases. Neither Kate nor myself has the stomach to keep our front row seats to the horrendous crimes we've seen. We want to focus on changing the communities before the crimes are committed. My wife still isn't admitting she's suffering from compassion fatigue and that's okay. All of my research tells me she'll be just fine as long as she takes time to care for herself. Spending time away from the office caring for our son and getting the much needed break she needs will be good for her. It's good for both of us. Since Jonah's birth, Nadine, Shamika, and Syreeta have spent countless hours fussing over our family. Ryan's wife Janice has joined in and for the first time in her life, Kate is getting the care and support she needs.

Landon McMurray, Detective Jennings, Nadine, Higgins, Ryan, and I have maintained contact in the weeks following the arrest of Thomas for his role in the gambling ring. The city of Charlotte moved away from the stories about Ron and Evan and spent weeks crucifying Thomas in the paper. The man that was elected to ensure the poor had adequate representation was using their lives as pawns in his chess match. The public outcry was severe. The mayor wasn't implicated, but her lack of oversight was called into question. Following an anonymous warning to her office regarding pictures of her and Thomas in bed together, she resigned. My team may not be made up of best friends, but we're all on the same page. We're dedicated to making sure the officials that run the city of Charlotte are doing what's in the best interest of the people, not their pockets.

Ryan

I awake to the feel of someone nudging my arm.

"Daddy's not ready to get up yet Kaitlin. It's Saturday."

"It's not Kaitlin."

I smile and turn to face my wife. Janice and I have worked hard on our marriage over the past couple of months. Ayers & Ayers has been an absolute madhouse with both Kate and Michael being out of the office, but I've made coming home and being present with my family a priority. Janice found an amazing therapist that has been counseling us both individually and together. It hasn't been easy, but it has been the most beneficial experience of our relationship.

I often shake my head at myself at how clueless I was to the true nature of our relationship. Janice spent years trying to please me and encourage me to be more engaged in the marriage. I spent that time thinking everything was perfect. I was blindsided and broken when I learned of her affair, but the truth is, it's probably the best thing that ever happened to us. I don't know if I'd still feel this way if she'd slept with him or if she still worked for him. Yet here in this moment, in these circumstances, I understand why things happened the way they did. I'm not happy they happened, but I finally understand.

"Are you coming down for breakfast? Kaitlin is already waiting."

"Why didn't you wake me sooner?" I ask as I pull my wife close to me. "We could have had some fun before she woke up."

"Oh no you don't," Janice teases as she pushes away from me. "You know we'll never get out of this bed if you start that this morning. Come on, we have a busy day planned. Kaitlin wants to go to the zoo."

I smile up at my wife as she stands and begins to leave the room. "Janice," I call out to her.

"Yes," she responds as she turns to face me looking more beautiful than I've ever seen her.

"I love you."